44m

Mr

£2.95 £2

G000254370

ff

FOUR STORIES

Rachel Ingalls

faber and faber
LONDON · BOSTON

First published in 1987
by Faber and Faber Limited
3 Queen Square London WC1N 3AU

Printed in Great Britain by
Richard Clay Ltd, Bungay, Suffolk
All rights reserved

British Library Cataloguing in Publication Data

Ingalls, Rachel
Four stories.
I. Title
813'.54[F]   PS3559.N38

ISBN 0-571-14546-9

Contents

I See a Long Journey

Flora had met James when she was going out with his younger brother, Edward. She'd been crazy about Edward, who even then had had a reputation for wildness where girls were concerned. She'd been eighteen, Edward nineteen. James was thirty-one.

She'd liked him straight away. He was easy in talking to her: relaxed and completely open, as if they'd known each other a long time. In fact, in a way she did know him already – not just through Edward, but from her older sister, Elizabeth, who had gone out with him for about two months a few years before. He had had many girlfriends and mistresses, naturally. He was agreeable and amusing, well known everywhere and well liked. He was also the most important of the heirs.

When he proposed to her, she thought her decision over carefully. She wasn't in love with him but she couldn't think of any reason why she should turn him down. He'd become such a good friend that she felt they were already related.

After the marriage, Edward changed along with everything else. The barriers came up all around her. Where once, on the outside, she had felt shut out of their exclusive family, now – on the inside – she was debarred from the rest of the world.

There had been a time at the beginning when she had fought. If it hadn't been for the money, she might have succeeded. Their quarrels, misunderstandings and jealousies were like those of other families. And she was like other girls who marry into a group of powerful personalities. She was tugged in different directions by all of them. They expected things of her. They criticized her. They tried to train and educate her. When she was pregnant for the first time, and when she had the child, they told her what she was doing wrong.

But that was the stage at which she found her own strength: she clung to the child and wouldn't let them near it. They had to make concessions. It was the first grandchild and a boy. She was sitting pretty. She could take her mother-in-law up on a point in conversation and make her back down.

Shortly after the birth a lot of pressure was taken off her anyway; Edward formed a liaison with a girl who sang in a nightclub. He was thinking of marrying her, he said. He wanted to introduce her to his parents – her name was Lula. His mother hit the roof about it. She described the girl as 'an unfortunate creature: some sort of half-breed, I believe'. Quarrels exploded over the breakfast table, down in the library, out in the garden. In the kitchen, of course, they were laughing.

She met Lula. Edward took them both out to lunch. Flora wasn't nervous about it: she even tried to put the other woman at her ease by saying she too had once been an outsider to the family. But Lula wasn't going to accept anyone's sympathy. She put on a performance, talked loudly, looking around at the other people in the restaurant, pinched Edward under the table and went out of her way to throw as many dirty words as possible into every sentence. Then she stood up abruptly, declared that it had been so very, very nice but she had to run along now, tugged Edward by the hair and left.

'She isn't like that,' he said.

'You don't have to tell me. I could see. She'll be all right when we get together next time.'

'She really isn't like that.'

'I know. I told you – I recognize the camouflage. I liked her fine.'

'I think you made her feel unsure.'

'And I'm the easy one. Wait till she meets the others. She'll have her work cut out for her.'

'They gave you a rough time, I guess.'

'It's all right. That's over now.'

'It's mainly Mother.'

'It's the whole deal.'

'But things are okay between you and James?'

'Oh, yes,' she said. 'But we're in the thick of everything. If you and I had married, we could have escaped together.'

'But we didn't love each other,' he said matter-of-factly. It upset her to hear him say it. Someone should love her. Even her children – they needed her, but she was the one who did the loving.

'Besides,' he told her, 'I'm not sure that I want to escape. Even if it were possible. And I don't think it is.'

'It's always possible if you don't have children.'

He said, 'It's the price of having quarterly cheques and dividends, never having to work for it. Think of the way most people live. Working in a factory – could you stand it?'

'Maybe it wouldn't be so bad. If you were with somebody you loved.'

'Love doesn't survive much poverty. Unless you're really right down at the bottom and don't have anything else.'

Was it true? If she and her husband were lost and wandering in the desert, maybe he'd trade her for a horse or a camel, because he could always get another wife and have more children by the new one. It couldn't be true.

'I'm sure it would,' she said.

'From the pinnacle, looking down,' he told her, 'you get that romantic blur. Wouldn't it be nice in a little country cottage with only the birds and the running streams? It's the Marie Antoinette complex.'

And at another time he'd said, 'Love is a luxury for us. If I were on a desert island with the soulmate of all time, I'd still have the feeling that I'd ducked out. I guess it's what they used to call "duty".'

'There are plenty of others to take over the duties,' she'd told him.

'And they'd all think: *he wasn't up to it*. And they'd be right.'

It took two years for the family to wean Edward away from Lula. Then they set him up with a suitable bride, an Irish heiress named Anna-Louise, whose family was half-German on the mother's side. One of Anna-Louise's greatest assets was that she was a superb horsewoman. Flora liked her. The boy's father, the old man, thought she was wonderful. His wife realized too late that Anna-Louise was a strong character, not to be bullied. Flora was let off the hook. She didn't allow her mother-in-law to take out on her or her children any of the failures and frustrations she had with Anna-Louise. She put her foot down. And eventually her mother-in-law came to her to seek an ally, to complain and to ask for advice. Flora listened and held her peace. She was learning.

James was the one who helped her. He guided her through her mistakes; he was the first person in her life to be able to teach her that mistakes are actually the best method of learning and that it's impossible to learn without at least some of them. He warned her about things she would have to know, strangers she was going to meet. She was grateful. But she also saw that he was part of the network and that all his actions, though well meant, were aimed at making her just like the rest of them, whether she wanted to be or not.

It always came down to the question of money. The money made the difference. They were one of the richest families on the Eastern seaboard. Flora's own parents were from nice, substantial backgrounds; they'd had their houses and companies and clubs, and belonged to the right places when it had still been worth keeping up with that sort of thing.

She'd known people who knew the cousins, who gave parties at which she would be acceptable – that was how she had met Edward. Everyone knew about them. Everyone recognized their pictures in the papers. To marry into their ranks was like marrying into royalty, and a royalty that never had to worry about its revenues.

Her marriage had also changed her own relatives irrevocably. It was as though they had lost their thoughts and wishes; they had become hangers-on. They name-dropped with everyone; they could no longer talk about anything except the last time they'd seen James or Edward or – best of all – the old man.

They were all corrupted. One early summer afternoon Flora sat playing cards with James and Edward and her sister, Elizabeth, who had married a cousin of the family and thus, paradoxically, become less close.

Flora thought about the four of them, what they were doing with the time they had. All except for James were still in their twenties and they were like robots attached to a master-computer – they had no ideas, no lives. They were simply parts of a machine.

She wondered whether James and Elizabeth had slept together long ago, before she had become engaged to him, and thought they probably had. An exhaustion came over her: the artificial weariness enforced upon someone who has many capabilities and is consistently prevented from using any of them.

The doctors called it depression. She worked on her tennis, went swimming three times a week, had helped to organize charity fund-raising events. She made progress. Now she was an elegant young matron in magazine pictures, not the messy-haired girl who had run shrieking down the hallway from her mother-in-law's room as she held her squealing baby in one arm and then slammed and locked the door after her. She would never again stay behind a locked door, threatening to cut her throat, to go to the newspapers, to get a divorce. James had stood on the other side of the door and talked to her for five hours until she'd given in.

And now they had their own happy family together and she moved through the round of public and domestic duties as calmly and gracefully as a swan on the water. But the serenity of her face was like the visible after-effect of an illness she had survived; or like a symptom of the death that was to follow.

James thought they should take their holiday in a spot more remote than the ones they usually chose in the winter. He was fed up with being hounded by reporters and photographers. And she was nervous about the children all the time. The house had always received a large quantity of anonymous mail and more than the average number of unpleasant telephone cranks. Now they were being persecuted not just because of their wealth, but because it was the fashion. Every day you could read in the papers about 'copy cat' crimes – acts of violence committed in imitation of something the perpetrators had seen on television or in the headlines of the very publication you had in your hand. If there had been a hoax call about a bomb at some large public building, it was fairly certain that the family secretaries would be kept busy with their share of telephone threats in the next few days. Everyone in the house was on speaking terms with at least ten policemen. There had been many crises over the years. They counted on the police, although James's mother, and his sister Margaret's ex-husband too, said they sometimes thought that most of the information these nuts and maniacs found out about them came straight from the police themselves.

Anna-Louise's entry into the family had brought further complications, adding an interest for the Irish connections on all sides. Anna-Louise herself wasn't afraid. She wasn't in any case the sort of woman who worried, but on top of that, her children hadn't been put in danger yet, whereas Margaret's had: her daughter, Amy, was once almost spirited away by a gang of kidnappers. 'Fortunately,' Margaret told friends later, 'they got the cook's niece instead. She was standing out at the side of the back drive, and it just shows how dumb these people are: it was

Sunday and she was wearing a little hat, white gloves, a pink organdie dress and Mary Janes. If they'd known anything about Amy, they'd have realized she wouldn't be caught dead in a get-up like that. As a matter of fact, at that time of day on a Sunday, she'd be in her jeans helping MacDonald in the greenhouses.'

They had paid handsomely to get the niece back; good cooks weren't easy to find. But they'd cooperated with the police, which they wouldn't have dared to do if Amy herself had been the victim: it would have been too big a risk, even though in that particular case it had worked and they had caught the three men and rescued the girl. Flora later began to think it would have been better for the niece not to have lived through the capture; she started to crack up afterwards and developed a bitter enmity towards Amy, who, she told everybody, ought to have been the one to be seized.

The incident had taken place when Flora was in the beginning months of her second pregnancy. It brought home to her how difficult it was to escape the family destiny: even the children were dragged into it. And though it was only one of the many frightening, uncomfortable or calamitous events from the background of her first few years of marriage, it was the one that turned her into a woman who fretted about the future and who, especially, feared for the safety of her children. James tried to soothe her. On the other hand, his friend and chauffeur, Michael, who kept telling her everything would be all right, seemed at the same time to approve of the fact that she worried. She thought he felt it was a proof that she was a good mother.

'If we go too far away,' she said to James, 'the children – '

'We'll have telephones and telegraphs, and an airport nearby. It isn't any worse than if we were going to California for the weekend.'

'But it's so far away.'

He asked, 'What could we do, even here, if anything happened?' The question was meant to mollify, but it scared her even more.

'The doctor says you need a rest,' he insisted. She agreed with that. It seemed odd that a woman should live in a house as large as a castle, with nothing to do all day but easy, pleasant tasks, and still need a rest. But it was true.

'Michael will be with us,' he added.

That, finally, convinced her. If Michael came along, nothing bad could happen, either at home or abroad. She was distrustful of even the smallest disruption to her life, but she wanted to go. And she would be relieved to get away from the menace of all the unknown thousands who hated her without even having met her.

You couldn't be free, ever. And if you were rich, you were actually less often free than other people. You were recognized. The spotlight was on you. Strangers sent you accusations, threats and obscene letters. And what had you done to them? Nothing. Even the nice people were falsified by the ideas they had of your life; those who didn't threaten begged. Everyone wanted money and most of them felt no shame at demanding it outright. They were sure they deserved it, so they had to have it. It didn't matter who gave it to them.

She too had been altered, of course. She had made her compromises and settled down. Of all the people connected with the family only Michael, she felt, had kept his innocence. His loyalty was like the trust of a child. When he drove her into town to shop, when they said hello or goodbye, she thought how wonderful it would be to put her arms around him, to have him put his arms around her. She was touched and delighted by all his qualities, even at the times when she'd seen him thwarted or frustrated and noticed how he went white and red very quickly.

'All right,' she said. 'If Michael comes too.'

'Of course,' James told her. 'I wouldn't be without him. There's a good hotel we can stay at. I don't think you'll need a maid.'

'I don't want a maid. I just want to be able to phone home twice a day to check if everything's all right.'

'Everything's going to be fine. You know, sometimes kids can get sick of their parents. It won't do them any harm to miss us for a week or two.'

'Two?'

'Well, if we don't make it at least two, half the trip's going to be spent in the plane, or recovering from jet-lag.'

They had parties to say goodbye: the friends' party, the relatives', and one birthday party for Margaret's youngest child, which coincided with a garden club meeting. Flora's mother-in-law directed the gloved and hatted ladies around flowerbeds that were to be mentioned in the yearly catalogue. Her father-in-law put in a brief appearance at the far end of the Italian gardens, shook hands with a few of the women and came back to the house, where he stayed for quite a while looking with delectation at the children digging into their ice cream and cake. Flora smiled at him across the table. She got along well with him, as did all his daughters-in-law, though Anna-Louise was his favourite. His own daughters had less of his benevolence, especially Margaret, whose whole life had been, and was still, lived in the always unsuccessful effort to gain from him the admiration he gave so freely to others. That was one of the family tragedies that Flora could see clearly. No one ever said anything about it and she'd assumed from the beginning that, having grown up with it, they'd never noticed. It was simply one more truth that had become acceptable by being ritualized.

The birthday room was filled with shouts and shrieks. Food was smeared, thrown and used to make decorations. One boy had built a palace of cakes and candies on his plate. There were children of industrialists, oil millionaires, ambassadors, bankers and heads of state; but they looked just like any other children, grabbing each other's paper hats while one of them was sick on the rug.

Michael too was looking on. He was enjoying himself, but he was there to work. He watched with a professional, noting glance. If anything went wrong, he was there to stop it. His presence made Flora feel safe and happy. She began to look forward to the trip.

The next evening, it was the grown-ups' turn to be sick on the rug. Five of their guests had to stay over for the weekend. On Monday morning Flora and James left for the airport.

At first she'd wanted to take hundreds of photographs with her. She'd started looking through the albums and every few pages taking one or two out; then it was every other page. Finally she had a fistful of pictures, a pile as thick as a doorstop. James chose twelve, shoved the others into a drawer and told her they had to hurry now.

The children waved and smiled, their nurse cried. 'I wish she wouldn't do that,' Flora said in the car. 'Bursting into tears all the time.'

'Just a nervous habit,' he told her. 'It doesn't seem to affect the kids. They're a pretty hard-bitten bunch.' He clasped his hand over hers, over the new ring he had given her the night before. She tried to put everything out of her mind, not to feel apprehensive about the plane flight.

They were at the airport with plenty of time to spare, so he took her arm and led her to the duty-free perfume, which didn't interest her.

'There's a bookstore,' she said.

'All right.'

They browsed through thrillers, war stories, romantic novels and books that claimed to tell people how society was being run and what the statistics about it proved.

They became separated. The first James knew of it was when he heard her laugh coming from the other side of the shop and saw her turn, looking for him. She was holding a large magazine.

'Come look,' she called. The magazine appeared to be some kind of colouring book for children. There was a whole shelf full of the things. After the paper people in the drawings were coloured and cut free, you snipped out the pictures of their clothes and pushed the tabs down over the shoulders of the dolls.

'Aren't they wonderful?' she said. 'Look. This one's called "Great Women Paper Dolls". It's got all kinds of . . . Jane Austen, Lady Murasaki, Pavlova. Look at the one of Beatrix Potter: she's got a puppy in her arms when she's in her fancy dress, but underneath it's a rabbit. And – '

'These are pretty good,' he said. He'd discovered the ones for boys: history, warfare, exploration. 'As a matter of fact, the text to these things is of a very high standard. Too high for a colouring book.'

'Paper doll books.'

'You've got to colour them before you cut them out. But anybody who could understand the information would be too old to want one. You wonder who they're aimed at.'

'At precocious children like ours, of course. They'll think they're hysterical. We can send them these. Paper dolls of Napoleon and Socrates. Look, it says here: if I don't see my favourite great woman, I may find her in the book called "Infamous Women Paper Dolls". Oh James, help me look for that one.'

'Flora,' he said, 'the children are here. We're the ones who are supposed to be going away.'

'Yes, but we can send them right now, from the airport. Aren't they funny? Look. Infamous Women – how gorgeous. Catherine di Medici, Semiramis. And in the other one – here: an extra dress for Madame de Pompadour; the only woman to get two dresses. Isn't that nice? She'd have appreciated that.'

She was winding herself up to the point where at any moment her eyes would fill with tears. He said, 'Who's that one? Looks like she got handed the castor oil instead of the free champagne.'

'Eadburga.'

'Never heard of her.'

'It says she was at her worst around 802. Please, James. We can leave some money with the cashier.'

'Anything to get you out of this place,' he told her.

After they'd installed themselves in their seats and were up in the air, he said, 'What was the difference between the great and the infamous?'

'The great were artists and heroic workers for mankind,' she said. 'The infamous were the ones in a position of power.'

The speed of her reply took him by surprise. He couldn't remember if it might have been true. Florence Nightingale, he recalled, had figured among the greats; Amelia Earhart, too. But there must also have been a ruler of some sort: Elizabeth I, maybe? Surely Queen Victoria had been in the book of good ones. And Eleanor of Aquitaine had been on a page fairly near that. He was still thinking about the question after Flora had already fallen asleep.

They arrived in an air-conditioned airport much like any other, were driven away in limousines with smoked-glass windows and were deposited at their hotel, where they took showers and slept. The first thing they did when they woke up was to telephone home. They didn't really look at anything until the next day.

They walked out of the marble-pillared hotel entrance arm in arm and blinked into the sun. They were still turned around in time. Already Flora was thinking about an afternoon nap. They looked to the left and to the right, and then at each other. James smiled and Flora pressed his arm. The trip had been a good idea.

They strolled slowly forward past the large, glittering shops that sold luxury goods. You could have a set of matching jade carvings packed and sent, jewellery designed for you, clothes tailored and completed in hours. James said, 'We can do all that later.' Flora stopped in front of a window display of jade fruit. She said, 'It's probably better to get it over with.'

They stood talking about it: whether they'd leave the presents till later and go enjoy themselves, or whether they ought to get rid of the duties first, so as not to have them hanging over their heads for two weeks. Michael waited a few feet to the side, watching, as usual, without seeming to.

They decided to do the difficult presents first – the ones that demanded no thought but were simply a matter of knowing what to ask for and choosing the best. They handed over credit cards and traveller's cheques for tea sets, bolts of silk material, dressing gowns, inlaid boxes, vases, bowls and bronze statuettes. By lunchtime they were worn out.

They went back to the hotel to eat. Light came into the high-ceilinged dining-room through blinds, shutters, curtains and screens. It was as if they were being shielded from an outside fire – having all the heat blocked out, while some of the light was admitted. About twenty other tables were occupied. Michael sat on his own, though if they had had their meal in town, he'd have eaten with them.

James looked around and smiled again. 'This is very pleasant,' he said. He beamed at her and added, 'I think the holiday is already doing its job. You're looking extremely well after all our shopping. Filled with a sense of achievement.'

'Yes, I'm okay now. Earlier this morning I was feeling a lot like Eadburga.'

'How's that?'

'At her worst around 8.15, or whenever it was.'

He laughed. It had taken her years to say things that made him laugh and she still didn't know what sort of remark was going to appeal to him. Sometimes he'd laugh for what seemed like no reason at all, simply because he was in the mood.

They went up to their rooms for a rest. She closed her eyes and couldn't sleep. He got up, shuffled through the magazines and newspapers he'd already read, and said he couldn't sleep, either. They spent the afternoon making love, instead.

'Dress for dinner tonight?' she asked as she arranged her clothes in the wardrobe.

'Let's go someplace simple. I've had enough of the well-tempered cuisine. Why don't we just slouch around and walk in somewhere?'

'You wouldn't rather get the ptomaine at the end of the trip rather than straight away?'

'Well, we've got lists of doctors and hospitals a mile long. We could get a shot for it.'

'Will Michael be coming with us?'

'Of course,' he said.

'Then I guess it's safe enough.'

'In a pinch, I could probably protect you, too.'

'But you might get your suit creased.' She made a funny face at him.

'I love vacations,' he told her. 'You're definitely at your best.'

'I told you: I'm fine now.'

'They say most of the jet-lag hangover is caused by dehydration, but the big difference I've noticed this time is the change in light.'

'Well, it's nice to be away for a while. There'll be at least three new quarrels going by the time we get back, and they'll be missing us a lot.'

'We might take more time off sometime. A long trip. A year or so.'

'Oh, Jamie, all the sweat. I couldn't do it so soon again, setting up a whole new household and uprooting the children from all their friends.'

'I didn't mean I'd be working. I meant just you and me away from everybody in a lovely spot, somewhere like Tahiti. New Caledonia, maybe.'

She said again, 'Would Michael come too?'

'I don't know. I hadn't thought.'

She pulled a dress out by the hanger and decided that it wasn't too wrinkled to wear without having the hotel maid iron it.

'I guess he'd have to,' James said.

'He wouldn't mind?'

'Kelvin? He never minds anything. He'd love to.'

She'd have to think. If it had been Michael asking her to go away with him to the South Seas, she'd have gone like a shot. But the more dissatisfied she'd become with her life, the more reluctant she was to make any changes.

She said, 'Well, it's something to think over. When would you want to make a decision about it?'

'Three weeks, about then.'

'All right. We'll have to talk about the children. That's the main thing.'

She was still worrying about the children as they started towards the steps that led to the elevators. There was an entire puzzle-set of interlocking staircases carpeted in pale green and accompanied by carved white banisters that made the whole arrangement look like flights of ornamental balconies. If you wanted to, you could continue on down by the stairs. James always preferred to ride in elevators rather than walk. Exercise, in his opinion, was what sport was for; it wasn't meant to move you from one place to another. Locomotion should be carried out with the aid of machines and servants.

'Let me just call home again quick,' she suggested.

'You'll wake them all up. It's the wrong time there.'

'Are you sure? I'm so mixed up myself, I can't tell.'

'We'll phone when we get back from supper,' he said.

They had been on other trips together long ago, when the telephoning had become a genuine obsession. Now they had a routine for it: she mentioned it, he told her when, she believed him and agreed to abide by the times he designated. The whole game was a leftover from the unhappy years when she'd had no self-confidence and felt that she kept doing everything wrong.

Michael stepped into the elevator after them. He moved behind them as they walked through the lobby.

'Look,' Flora said.

The central fountain, which earlier in the day had been confined to three low jets, now sprayed chandelier-like cascades of brilliance into the three pools beneath. Tables and chairs had been set out around the display and five couples from the hotel were being served tea. As Flora and James watched, a group of children rushed for a table, climbed into the chairs and began to investigate the spoons and napkins. A uniformed nurse followed them.

James said, 'Like some tea?'

'Unless Michael doesn't – '

'Sure,' Michael said. 'I'll sit right over there.' He headed towards the sofas and armchairs near the reception desk. Wherever they were, he always knew where to find the best spots for surveillance, and probably had a good idea where everybody else might choose to be, too. He'd been trained for all that. You couldn't see from his walk or from the way his clothes fitted that he carried guns and a knife, but he did. Sometimes it seemed incredible to Flora that he had been through scenes of violence; he'd been in the marines for two years while James was finishing up college. His placid, law-abiding face gave no sign of the fact. But she thought how upsetting the experience must

have been to him at first. Even killing didn't come naturally –
especially killing: somebody had to teach it to you. And boys
weren't really cruel or bloodthirsty unless they had a background
of brutality.

Michael's background, she knew, was quite ordinary. He was
a child of an undergardener and one of the parlourmaids at the
house. Once she'd asked him how he'd managed to get through
his military training and he'd told her that he'd been lucky: he'd
been with a group of boys who'd become really good friends.
And, as for violence, he'd added, 'You got to be objective, say to
yourself this is completely a professional thing. Like render unto
Caesar. You know?' She had nodded and said yes, but had had
no idea what he'd been talking about.

They sat close enough to the fountain to enjoy it but not so near
as to be swept by the fine spray that clouded its outpourings.
James had also taken care to station himself, and her, at a
reasonable distance from the children, who looked like more
than a match for their wardress.

Their nearest companions were a man and a woman who
might have been on a business trip or celebrating an early
retirement. They gave the impression of being a couple who had
been married for a long time. The woman looked older than the
man. She had taken two extra chairs to hold her shopping bags
and as soon as the tea was poured out she began to rummage
through her papers and packages. She looked up and caught
Flora's eye. Flora smiled. The woman said, 'I couldn't resist. It's
all so pretty and the prices are just peanuts. Aren't they,
Desmond?'

The man's eyes flicked to the side. 'We're going to need an
extra plane to take it all back,' he said. His head turned to the
stairway and the main door, warily, as if looking for eavesdroppers.

'Not here,' his wife told him.

'Only damn part of this hotel they let you smoke a pipe is in
your own room. Place must be run by the anti-tobacco league.'

'Do you good,' his wife said. She began to talk about silks and
jade and porcelain. Flora guessed before the woman started to
quote numbers that they were going to be several price-brackets
under anything she and James would have bought. On the other
hand, like most rich people, she loved hunting down bargains.

The couple, whose name was Dixon, went on to tell their
opinions of the city and of the country in general. They regretted,

they said, not having made provision for trips outside town to – for example – the big flower festival that had been held the week before, or just the ordinary market mornings. They were leaving the next day. Flora saw James relax as he heard them say it: there wasn't going to be any danger of involvement. He began to take an interest in the list of places and shops they recommended. Flora was halfway through her second cup of tea and could tell that James would want to leave soon, when Mrs Dixon said, 'What I regret most of all, of course, is that we never got to see the goddess.'

'Oh,' Flora said. 'At the festival?'

'At her temple.'

'A statue?'

'No, no. That girl. You know – the one they train from childhood, like the Lama in Tibet.'

'Not like that,' her husband said.

'Well, I just couldn't face standing in line for all that time in the heat. But now I really wish I'd given myself more of a push.'

'I haven't heard about the goddess,' Flora admitted. James said that he'd read about it somewhere, he thought, but only remembered vaguely. And he hadn't realized that the custom had to do with this part of the world.

'Oh, yes,' Mr Dixon told him, and launched into the history of the goddess, who was selected every few years from among thousands of candidates. The child was usually four or five years old when chosen, had to be beautiful, to possess several distinct aesthetic features such as the shape of the eyes and ears and the overall proportion of the limbs, and could have no blemish. 'Which is quite an unusual thing to be able to find,' he said. 'Then – '

'Then,' Mrs Dixon interrupted, 'they train her in all the religious stuff and they also teach her how to move – sort of like those temple dancers, you know: there's a special way of sitting down and getting up, and holding out your fingers, and so on. And it all means something. Something religious. There are very strict rules she's got to obey about everything – what she can eat and drink, all that. Oh, and she should never bleed. If she cuts herself – I forget whether she has to quit or not.'

'She just has to lie low for a few days, I think,' Mr Dixon said.

'And she can never cry – did I say that?'

'And never show fear.'

'Then at puberty – '

'She's out on her can and that's the whole ball game. They go and choose another one.'

'So people just drive out to her temple to look at her,' Flora asked, 'as if she's another tourist attraction?'

'Oh no, dear,' Mrs Dixon said. 'They consult her. They take their troubles to her and she gives them the solution. It's like an oracle. And I think you donate some small amount for the upkeep of the temple. They don't mind tourists, but it isn't a show – it's a real religious event.'

Mr Dixon said, 'She's very cultivated, so it seems. Speaks different languages and everything.'

James asked, 'What happens to her afterwards?'

'Oh, that's the joke. She used to spend the rest of her life in seclusion as the ex-goddess. But this last time, the girl took up with a young fellow, and now she's married to him and – '

' – and there's the most terrific scandal,' Mrs Dixon said happily. 'It's really turned things upside-down. I guess it's like a priest getting married to a movie star. They can't get over it.'

'Matter of fact, I wouldn't want to be in that girl's shoes.'

'Why?' Flora asked.

Mr Dixon shrugged. 'A lot of people are mad as hell. They've been led to expect one thing and now this other thing is sprung on them. They're used to thinking of their goddess as completely pure, and also truly sacred. I guess it can't look right for her to revert to being human all of a sudden, just like the rest of us. See what I mean?'

Flora nodded.

'She's broken the conventions,' James said, which didn't seem to Flora nearly such a good explanation as Mr Dixon's, but she smiled and nodded again.

They took a long time deciding where they wanted to eat their evening meal. In the beginning it was too much fun looking around to want to go inside; they had discovered the night life of the streets, full of people going about ordinary business that might have taken place indoors during the daytime: there were open-air barber shops, dress stalls where customers could choose their materials and be measured for clothes; shops that stocked real flowers and also stands that sold bouquets made out of feathers and silk.

'No wonder Mrs Dixon had all those piles of packages,' Flora said. 'Everything looks so nice.'

'Under this light,' James warned. 'I bet it's pretty tacky in daylight.'

Michael grunted his assent.

'Don't you think it's fun?' she asked.

'Very colourful,' he said. She wasn't disappointed in his answer. It gave her pleasure just to be walking beside him.

She would have liked to eat in one of the restaurants that were no more than just a few tables and chairs stuck out on the sidewalk. James vetoed the suggestion. They moved back to the beginning of richer neighbourhoods and he suddenly said, 'That one.'

In front of them was a building that looked like a joke: dragons and pagodas sprouting everywhere from its rooftops. The lower floor was plate glass, which reassured the three of them – that looked modern and therefore unromantic and probably, they expected, hygienic. 'We can rough it for once,' James said. Through the downstairs windows they could see rows of crowded booths, people sitting and eating. Most of the patrons appeared to be tourists – another good sign.

They entered and were seated all on the same side of a table. Flora had hoped to be put between the two men, but the waiter had positioned Michael at James's far side. Opposite her an old man was eating noodles from a bowl. He stared determinedly downward.

They looked at the menu. As James ordered for them, a young couple came up and were shown to the remaining places; he had a short beard and wore a necklace consisting of a single wooden bead strung on a leather thong; she had a long pigtail down her back. They were both dressed in T-shirts and blue jeans and carried gigantic orange back-packs. They made a big production of taking off the packs and resting them against the outside of the booth. When the old man on the inside had finished eating and wanted to get out, they had to go through the whole routine again. Once they were settled, they stared across the table contemptuously at the fine clothes the others were wearing. They seemed to be especially incredulous over James's outfit, one which he himself would have considered a fairly ordinary linen casual suit for the tropics.

James switched from English to French and began to tell Flora about New Caledonia. It meant that Michael was excluded from the conversation, but he knew that this was one of James's favourite methods of detaching himself from company he didn't want to be associated with. It only worked in French because Flora's limited mastery of other languages wouldn't permit anything else. James had always been good at learning new languages. As a child he had even made up a language that he and Michael could use to baffle grown-up listeners. Occasionally they spoke it even now. Flora had figured out that it must be some variation of arpy-darpy talk, but it always went so fast that she could never catch anything.

The back-packers spoke English. He was American, she Australian. Their names were Joe and Irma. They spent their whole time at the table discussing the relative merits of two similar articles they had seen in different shops. Some part of the objects had been made out of snakeskin and, according to Irma, one of them was 'pretty ratty-looking'; on the other one, so Joe claimed, the so-called snake had been an obvious fake, definitely plastic.

'It's like those beads you got,' he said. 'Supposed to be ivory, and you can see the join where they poured it into the mould in two halves and then stuck them together. Why can't you tell? How can you miss seeing it? If you keep on spending money like this—'

Irma muttered, 'Well, it's my money.'

'We should be keeping some by for emergencies,' he said. She sulked for the rest of the meal. She chewed her food slowly and methodically. Flora wished the girl had picked everything up, thrown it all over her companion and told him to go to hell. He was staring around with disapproving interest at the other diners. He wasn't going to feel guilty about hurting his girlfriend; he hadn't even noticed her play for sympathy.

Flora said in French, 'Could you really go for a year without work?'

'Sure. I'd work on something else,' James said. 'We'd get a nice boat, sail around.' He added, 'The food isn't too bad here.'

'Wait till tomorrow to say it,' she told him.

The weather next morning looked like being the start of another wonderful day. All the days were wonderful in that climate at the right time of year. They both felt fine. Michael too said he was okay. Flora called home.

She got Margaret on the line, who said, 'We've missed you. Anna-Louise is on the warpath again.'

'What about?'

Anna-Louise's voice came in on an extension, saying, 'That isn't Margaret getting her story in first, is it? Flora?'

'Hi,' Flora said. 'How are you all?'

'The natives are restless, as usual.'

Margaret tried to chip in but was told by Anna-Louise to get off the line. There was a click.

'Children all right?' Flora asked.

'Couldn't be better.'

'Are they there?' She waved James over. They spent nearly fifteen minutes talking to the children, who said again how much they loved the paper doll books and how all their friends thought they were great and wanted some too. James began to look bored and to make motions that the conversation should stop. He leaned over Flora. 'We've got to hang up now,' he said into the mouthpiece.

They were the second couple into the breakfast room. 'Are we that early?' she asked.

He checked his watch. 'Only a little. It's surprising how many people use their holidays for sleeping.'

'I guess a lot of them have jet-lag, too. That's the trouble with beautiful places – they're all so far away.'

He spread out the maps as Michael was seated alone at a table for two several yards beyond them. Flora had them both in view, Michael and James. She felt her face beginning to smile. At that moment she couldn't imagine herself returning from the trip. The children and relatives could stay at the other end of the telephone.

James twitched the map into place. He liked planning things out and was good at it. She, on the other hand, couldn't even fold a map back up the right way. She was better at the shopping. Now that they were used to their routines, they had a better time sightseeing. In the early days James had spent even more time phoning his broker than Flora had in worrying about the babies.

She remembered the young couple at dinner the night before, and how much they had seemed to dislike each other. Of course, it was hard to tell anything about people who were quarrelling; still, they didn't seem to have acquired any of the manners and formulae and pleasing deceptions that helped to keep lovers

friendly over long periods, She herself had come to believe that –
if it weren't for this other glimpse of a love that would be for ever
unfulfilled – she'd have been content with just those diplomatic
gestures, plus a shared affection for what had become familiar. If
she had been free to choose at this age, her life would have been
different. Everybody was free now; and they all lived together
before they got married.

James put a pencil mark on the map and started to draw a line
across two streets.

Maybe, she thought, she'd been free even then. The freedom,
or lack of it, was simply ceremonial. Rules and customs kept you
from disorder and insecurity, but they also regulated your life to
an extent that was sometimes intolerable. They protected and
trapped at the same time. If it weren't for habit and codes of
behaviour, she and Michael could have married and had a happy
life together.

It had taken her years to find out that most of her troubles had
been caused by trying to switch from one set of conventions to
another. The people around her – even the ones who had at first
seemed to be against her – had actually been all right.

She said, 'You know what I'd really like to do? I'd like to see
that girl.'

'Hm?'

'The one the Dixons were talking about at tea. The goddess.'

'Oh.' James looked up. 'Well, maybe. But don't you think the
idea is going to be a lot better than the reality? Following it up is
just going to mean what they said: standing in line for hours. Do
you want to spend your vacation doing that?'

'And if you don't, regretting that you never did. I would like to.
Really. You don't have to come, if you don't want to.'

'Of course I'd come, if you went.'

'Could you find out about it? It's the thing I want to do most.'

'Why?'

'Why? Are there goddesses at home?'

He laughed, and said, 'Only in the museums. And in the
bedroom, if you believe the nightgown ads.'

'Please.'

'Okay,' he promised. 'I'll find out about it. But it seems to me,
the one worth looking at is going to be the one that went AWOL
and got married.'

'She didn't go AWOL. She was retired.'

'A retired goddess? No such thing. Once a god, always a god.'

'If you become impure as soon as you bleed, then you can lose the divinity. Women – '

'All right, I'll find out about it today. Right now. This very minute.'

'I'm only trying to explain it.'

'Wasted on me,' he told her.

'Don't you think it's interesting?'

'Mm.'

'What does that mean?'

'I'll see about it this afternoon.'

Over the next few days they went to the botanical gardens; to the theatre, where they saw a long, beautiful and rather dull puppet play; and to a nightclub, at which Flora developed a headache from the smoke and James said he was pretty sure the star *chanteuse* was a man. They got dressed up in their evening clothes to visit the best restaurant in town, attended a dinner given by a friend of the family who used to be with the City Bank in the old days, and made an excursion to the boat market. Half the shops there were hardly more than floating bamboo frameworks with carpets stretched across them. Bright pink orchid-like flowers decorated all the archways and thresholds, on land and on the water. The flowers looked voluptuous but unreal, and were scentless; they added to the theatrical effect – the whole market was like a view backstage. James and Flora loved it. Michael said it was too crowded and the entire place was a fire-trap.

'Well, there's a lot of water near at hand,' James said.

'You'd never make it. One push and the whole mob's going to be everybody on top of theirselves. They'd all drown together.'

'I do love it when you get on to the subject of safety, Kelvin. It always makes me feel so privileged to be alive.'

A privilege granted to many, Flora thought, as she gazed into the throng of shoving, babbling strangers. She suddenly felt that she had to sit down.

She turned to James. 'I feel – ' she began.

He saw straight away what was wrong. He put his arm around her and started to push through the crowd. Michael took the other side. She knew that if she really collapsed, Michael could pick her up and sling her over his shoulder like a sack of flour, he was so strong. He'd had to do it once when she'd fainted at a ladies' fund-raising luncheon. That had been a hot day too, lunch with wine under a blue canvas awning outdoors; but she'd been pregnant then. There was no reason now for her to faint, except the crowd and the lack of oxygen.

There wasn't any place to sit down. She tried to slump against Michael. They moved her forward.

'Here,' James said.

She sat on something that turned out to be a tea chest. They were in another part of the main arcade, in a section that sold all kinds of boxes and trunks. A man came up to James, wanting to know if he was going to buy the chest.

Back at the hotel, they laughed about it. James had had to shell out for a sandalwood casket in order to give her time to recover. When they were alone, he asked if she was really all right, or could it be that they'd been overdoing it in the afternoons? She told him not to be silly: she was fine.

'I think maybe we should cancel the trip to the goddess, though, don't you?'

'No, James. I'm completely okay.'

'Waiting out in the sun – '

'We'll see about that when we get there,' she said flatly. It was a tone she very seldom used.

'Okay, it's your vacation. I guess we could always carry you in on a stretcher and say you were a pilgrim.'

He arranged everything for the trip to the temple. The day he chose was near the end of their stay, but not so close to the flight that they couldn't make another date if something went wrong. One of them might come down with a twenty-four-hour bug or there might be a freak rainstorm that would flood the roads. 'Or,' James said, 'if she scratches herself with a pin, we've had it till she heals up. They might even have to choose a new girl.'

In the meantime they went to look at something called 'the jade pavilion' – a room in an abandoned palace, where the silk walls had been screened by a lattice-work fence of carved jade flowers. The stone had been sheared and sliced and ground to such a fineness that in some places it appeared as thin as paper. The colours were vibrant and glowing – not with the freshness of real flowers nor the sparkle of faceted jewels, but with the lustre of fruits; the shine that came off the surfaces was almost wet-looking.

As they walked under the central trellis a woman behind them said, 'Think of having to dust this place.' A man's voice answered her, saying, 'Plenty of slave labour here. Nobody worries about dust.'

'Glorious,' James said afterwards. And Michael declared that, 'You had to hand it to them.' He'd been impressed by the amount of planning that must have gone into the work: the measuring and matching, the exactitude.

Flora had liked the silk walls behind, which were covered with pictures of flying birds. She said, 'I guess you're supposed to think to yourself that you're in a garden, looking out. But it's a little too ornate for me. It's like those rooms we saw in Palermo, where the whole place was gold and enamel – like being inside a jewel box. This one would have been even nicer made out of wood and then painted. Don't you think?'

'That would fade,' James said. 'You'd have to re-do it all the time. And in this climate you'd probably need to replace sections of it every few years.'

They kept calling home every day. The weather there was horrible, everyone said. Anna-Louise had a long story about friends of hers whose house had been burgled. And one of the children had a sore throat; he coughed dramatically into the receiver to show how bad it was.

'They need us,' Flora said. 'That was a cry of despair.'

'That was the standard performance,' James told her. 'There's one who hasn't inherited any bashfulness. He'd cough his heart out in front of fifty reporters every day and do retakes if he thought it hadn't been a really thorough job. No hired substitute for him. It's going to be a question of how hard we'll have to sit on him to keep him down. Worse than Teddy was at that age.'

'He sounded pretty bad.'

'You're the one we're going to worry about at the moment. One at a time. Feeling faint? Claustrophobic?'

Flora shook her head. She felt fine. They strolled around town together and sat in a public park for a while. They'd chosen a bench within the shade of a widely branched, symmetrical tree. Michael rested against the stonework of a gate some distance away. While he kept them in sight, he watched the people who passed by. James pointed out a pair of tourists coming through the entrance.

'Where?' Flora asked.

'Right by the gate. It's those two from the restaurant we went to our first night out.'

'Irma and Joe,' she said. 'So it is. And they're still arguing. Look.'

The couple had come to a stop inside the gates. Joe leaned forward and made sweeping gestures with his arms. Irma held herself in a crouching position of defence: knees bent, shoulders hunched, chin forward. Her fists were balled up against her collar-bone. The two faced each other still encumbered by their back-packs and bearing a comical resemblance to armoured warriors or wrestlers costumed in heavy padding.

James said, 'She's just spent all her money and he's bawling her out.'

'You give it to him, Irma,' Flora said. James squeezed her hand.

They stayed on their bench and watched a large group of uniformed schoolchildren who – under the supervision of their teachers – went through what seemed to be the usual class exercises and then began to play some game neither Flora nor James could understand. Two of the children passed a book through the group while the others counted, telling off certain players to skip in a circle around the rest. Then they all sang a rhyming verse and formed up in a new order.

At last he said, 'Okay?' and stood up. She got to her feet. In the distance Michael too stepped forward.

They were three streets from where the hired car was parked, when Flora caught sight of a yellow bowl in a store window. She slowed down and, briefly, paused to look. James and Michael moved on a few paces. She turned back, to ask James what he thought about the bowl, and a hand closed gently over her arm just above the wrist. She looked up into a face she'd never seen before. For a moment she didn't realize anything. Then the hand tightened. At the same time, someone else grabbed her from behind. She dropped her handbag. Gasping and mewing sounds came from her throat, but she couldn't make any louder noise. She tried to kick, but that was all she could do.

Michael and James were with her almost immediately, hitting and kicking. Michael actually threw one of the gang into the air. Flora felt herself released. She fell to her knees, with her head against the glass of the window.

'Here,' James said, 'hold on to that.' He thrust her handbag into her arms and pulled her back up. She still couldn't speak. They hurried her to the car and drove back to the hotel.

Michael came up to the room with them and sat on the edge of the bed. James said he was calling in a doctor.

'I'm all right,' she jabbered, 'all right, perfectly – I'm fine. I'm just so mad. I'm so mad I could chew bricks. The nerve of those people!' She was shaking.

Michael stood up and got her a glass of water. She drank all of it and put her head down on the bed.

'That's a good idea,' James said. He and Michael left her and went into the sitting room. She could hear them talking. Michael said, 'The cops?' and James said, 'Tied up with police on vacation. Besides, what good?'

'No hope,' Michael answered. 'Anyway, weren't after money.'

'Bag.'

'No, arm. And left it. Her, not the. Alley right next. A few more seconds.'

'Jesus Christ,' James said. 'That means.'

Michael's voice said, 'Maybe not,' and Flora began to relax. She slept for a few minutes. She was on the beach in New Caledonia and Michael was sitting beside her on the sand. There was a barrel-vaulted roof of palm leaves overhead, like the canopy of a four-poster bed. She could hear the sound of the sea. And then suddenly someone stepped up in back of her and her arms were grabbed from behind.

She woke up. She almost felt the touch still, although it had been in her dream. She stared ahead at the chairs by the bed, the green-and-yellow pattern of the material they were upholstered in, the white net curtains over the windows where the light was beginning to dim away. She thought about the real event, earlier in the afternoon, and remembered again – as if it had left a mark on her body – the moment when the hand closed over her arm. Once more she was filled with outrage and fury. *The nerve*, she thought; *the nerve*. And the terrible feeling of having been made powerless, of being held, pinioned, captured by people who had no right to touch her. That laying of the hand on her had been like the striking of a predator, and just as impersonal. When she thought about it, it seemed to her that she was picturing all the men as much bigger and stronger than they probably were, and perhaps older, too. They might have been only teenagers.

She wanted to forget about it. It was over. And James was right: it would ruin what was left of their trip to spend it making out reports in a police station. What could the police do? These gangs of muggers hit you, disappeared around a corner and that was the end of the trail. Once in Tokyo she and James had seen a man on the opposite sidewalk robbed by two boys. His hands had suddenly gone up in the air; and there was the pistol right in broad daylight, pointing into his chest. It could happen so fast. It was the kind of street crime she had come on the holiday in order to forget.

But you had to be prepared. These things were international. And timeless. All the cruelties came back: torture, piracy, massacres. The good things didn't return so often because it took too long to develop them. And it took a whole system of convention and ritual to keep them working; wheels within wheels. She was part of it. To keep the ordered world safe, you had to budget for natural deterioration and the cost of replacement. Nothing had a very high survival rate – not even jade, hard as it was.

She thought about the pavilion of jade flowers and wondered whether it was really so beautiful. Maybe in any case it was only as good as the people who liked it believed it to be. James had loved it. Michael hadn't seemed to like it except for the evidence of the work that had been put into it. He might have disapproved of the extravagance rather than been judging the place on aesthetic grounds. She felt herself falling asleep again.

When she woke it was growing dark. She got up, took a shower and changed. The three of them ate together in the hotel dining-room, drank a great deal, had coffee and then even more to drink afterwards. They talked about law and order and decent values and Flora was tight enough to say, 'We can afford to.' They agreed not to mention the incident to anyone at home until the trip was over.

James had a hangover the next day but read through all his newspapers as usual.

'Any mention of our little drama?' she asked.

'Of course not. We didn't report it. A few other muggings here, it says.'

'Maybe they're the same ones.'

'Nope. They'd have gone for the bag and left you. These are all cases of grab-and-run.'

'You mean, they wanted to kidnap me; get you to pay a ransom. So, they must know all about us, who we are, what you can raise at short notice.'

'Maybe they check up on everybody staying at big hotels. Maybe they saw your rings. Or it might just be that they know a good-looking woman when they see one: probably thought they could sell you to somebody.'

'What?'

'Sure. Hey, look what else. It says here, the ex-goddess was stoned outside her house yesterday morning.'

'Yesterday morning we were pretty stoned, too. Or was that this morning?'

'A mob threw stones at her. They were some kind of religious group.'

'That's disgusting. That's even worse than trying to kidnap people.'

'She's all right, but she's in the hospital. That ought to mean she's okay. It only takes one stone to kill somebody.'

'Disgusting,' Flora muttered.

'And interesting,' James said. 'In a lot of countries it's still the traditional punishment for adultery.'

Their hired car drove them down the coastline. They took a picnic lunch, went for a swim and visited two shrines that, according to their guidebooks, were famous. On the next day they spent the morning trying to find material for curtains to go in a house belonging to Elizabeth's mother-in-law. Michael kept close to Flora all the time; their clothes often brushed as they walked or stood side by side.

On the day of their visit to the goddess it looked for the first time during the trip as if it might rain. James went back up to their rooms and got the umbrellas. On the ride out into the country they heard a few rumblings of thunder, but after that the skies began to clear and the day turned hot and muggy. The umbrellas sat in the car while they entered the temple precincts.

They were checked at the main gate, which looked more like the entrance to a fortress than to a religious building. Flora saw James stiffen as he caught sight of the long row of invalids sitting or lying on their sides, their relatives squatting near them on the ground. She remembered his joke about pilgrims. It wasn't so funny to see the real thing. He never liked being in places where there might be diseases. Most of their travelling had been carefully packaged and sanitized to avoid coming into contact with contagion or even the grosser aspects of simple poverty.

You could have all the shots you liked, and it wouldn't help against the wrong virus. She knew that he'd be telling himself again about the number and quality of the hospitals in town.

The officials looked at their papers, spoke to the driver and interpreter, and let them in. The pilgrims stayed outside on the ground. Flora wondered how long they'd have to wait, and how important it was to pay over money before you were granted an interview; or maybe the goddess did a kind of group blessing from a distance. If she wasn't even allowed to bleed, she might not be any more eager than James to get close to the diseased masses. Even when inside the courtyard you could hear a couple of them from over the wall, coughing their lungs out. The smell of decay that hung around the place might have been coming from the same source.

They were escorted across a vast, open space, through an archway, into another courtyard, across that, and to a third. The long-robed official then led them up on to the porch of one of the side buildings, around the verandah and into an assembly hall. It felt dark and cool after the walk in the open. About seventy people waited inside, some sitting on the floor and others – mainly Western tourists – either on the built-in wood bench that ran around three of the walls, or on fold-up seats they'd brought with them. There were also low stools you could borrow or rent from the temple.

The official swept forward towards a door at the far end of the hall. Two more robed figures stood guard by it. Flora's glance flickered lightly over the other people as she passed. There weren't many children there, except for very small babies that had had to be taken along so the mother could feed them. Most of the believers or curiosity-seekers were grown up and a good proportion of them quite old. A lot of them were also talking, the deaf ones talking loudly. Perhaps the fact that one figure was on its own, not turned to anyone else, was what made Flora notice: there, sitting almost in the middle of the dark wooden floor, was Irma, resting her spine against her back-pack. Joe wasn't with her. And she looked defeated, bedraggled, lost. Maybe she'd come not because this was a tourist attraction, but because she needed advice. She still looked to Flora like the complete guru-chaser – one of those girls who went wandering around looking for somebody to tell them the meaning of life. Yet she also looked desperate in another way, which Flora thought might not have anything to do with religion or philosophy or breaking up with a boyfriend, and might simply be financial. She was so struck by the girl's attitude that she almost forgot about the goddess.

They were rushed onward. The sentries opened the double doors for them and they went through like an awaited procession, entering and leaving three more hallways, all empty and each quieter than the last, until they reached a room like a schoolroom full of benches, they were asked to sit down. Their officials stepped forward to speak with two middle-aged priestesses who had come out of the chamber beyond – perhaps the place where the goddess was actually sitting. The idea suddenly gave Flora the creeps. It was like visiting a tomb.

She whispered to James, 'Did you see Irma out there?'

'Yes.'

'I'm glad she's split up with him, but she looks terrible. I think she must be broke.'

'Probably.'

'I'd like to give her something.'

'No.'

'Not much, just – '

It would mean so little to them, Flora thought, and so much to the girl. It would be even better to be able to tell her she'd done the right thing in leaving that boy and could choose a different man now if she wanted to, and this time find one who'd really love her.

James said, 'You've got to let people lead their own lives.'

Of course, it was assuming a lot. Irma might not have broken up with Joe at all. They might be meeting again in the evening after seeing the sights separately. Even so, it was certainly true that she had run out of money. There had to be some way of helping her out, but Flora couldn't think of one. Could she just hand over some cash and say, 'Did you drop this?' Maybe she could say, 'We were in the restaurant that night and you must have left this behind, it was lying in the corner of the seat and we've been looking for you ever since.'

'She'll fall on her feet,' James told her.

'For heaven's sake. It looks like she's fallen on her head. Can't we do something?'

'I don't think so. And I don't think we should. But if you still feel the same after we get through with this, we'll see. You'll have to figure out how to work it. And don't invite her back in the car.'

Flora stared upward, thinking. She saw for the first time that the ceiling beams were carved at regular intervals with formal designs and they were painted in colours so bright that they looked like enamelwork. She'd been right; that kind of thing was much more interesting than the jade pavilion. She thought: *I'll just put some bills into an envelope and use the story about finding it in the restaurant*. It was a shame when people ignored their good intentions because it was too difficult or too embarrassing to carry them out. She usually kept a few envelopes in her pocketbook.

The interpreter came back to their bench. 'Who is the seeker of truth?' he asked.

Flora looked blank. James said, 'What?'

'Is it you both two or three ask the goddess, or how many?'

'Just one,' James said. 'My wife.'

The man withdrew again. He spoke to the priestesses. One of them clapped her hands, the other went into the next room. The robed official spoke.

'Arise, if you please,' the interpreter told them. Michael moved from his bench to stand behind James. The three of them stepped forward until the official put up his hand against them.

The priestess came out again, leading a procession of eight women like herself. They walked two by two. In the middle of the line, after the first four and in front of the next four they'd kept a free space, in which trotted a midget-like, pink-clad figure: the goddess herself.

She was like a ceremonial doll only taken out on special occasions. Her robes reached to the floor. On her head she wore an elaborate triple-tiered crown of pearls and rubies and some sparkling greyish glass studs that were probably old diamonds. Long, wide earrings dangled from her ears and continued the framing lines of the ornamentation above, so that the still eyes seemed to float among the shimmering lights of crown, earrings, side panels and many-stranded necklaces.

All dressed up, just like a little lady, Flora thought; *what a dreadful thing to do to that child*. And yet the face that gazed out of all its glittering trappings was not exactly that of a child: enormous, dark eyes; serenely smiling mouth; the lovely bone-structure and the refinement of the features were like those of a miniature woman, not a child. Above all, the look of utter calmness and wisdom were strange to see. The girl could have been somewhere between seven and eight years old, although she was about the size of an American child of five.

The procession stopped. The official beckoned to Flora. She came up to where he pointed. The child, who hadn't looked at anything particular in the room, turned to her with pleased recognition, like a mother greeting a daughter.

Flora bowed and smiled back, slightly flustered but tingling with gratification. *This is weird*, she thought. *This is ridiculous*. But as the procession wheeled around, heading back into the room it had come from and gathering her along with it, she knew she would follow wherever they went and for however long they wanted her to keep going. She was actually close to tears.

The room was not a room, only another corridor. They had to walk down several turnings until they emerged at a courtyard of fruit trees. They entered the audience chamber from the far side.

The goddess seated herself on a wooden throne raised on steps. Like the rafters in this room too, the throne was carved and painted. She sat on a cushion of some ordinary material like burlap, which made her robes appear even more luxurious by contrast. Her tiny feet in their embroidered magenta slippers rested on one of the steps.

A robed woman, who had been waiting for them in the room, came and stood behind and a little to the side of the throne like a governess or a chaperone. Flora wondered if in fact the woman was to be the one to hand out the answers.

The little girl smiled prettily and said, 'Please sit.' She indicated the hassock in front of the steps to the throne. Flora knelt. She was uncomfortable. Her skirt felt too tight and her heart was thumping heavily. She raised her glance to the child and met, from out of all the silks and jewels, a look of happy repose.

'Speak freely,' the child told her in a musical voice. 'And say what is in your heart.'

Flora swallowed. She could hear the loud sound it made in her throat. All at once tears were in her eyes. She saw the figure before her in a blur, as if it might have been a holy statue and not a human being.

She began, 'I don't know what to do. Year after year. My life is useless. I have everything, nothing to want. Kind husband, wonderful children. I feel ashamed to be ungrateful, but it never was what . . . it never seemed like mine. It's as if I'd never had my own self. But there's one thing: a man. He's the only one who isn't corrupted, the only one I can rely on. I think about him all the time. I can't stop. I can't stand the idea that we'll never be together. He's only a servant. And I don't know what to do. I love him so much.' She ended on a sob and was silent.

She waited. Nothing happened. She sniffed, wiped the back of her hand across her cheek and looked up for her answer.

'Love?' the goddess asked.

Flora nodded. 'Yes,' she mumbled. 'Yes, yes.'

'True love', the sweet voice told her, 'is poor.'

Poor? Flora was bewildered. *Pure*, she thought. *Of course*.

'It's from the sky.'

The chaperone leaned forward towards the jewelled head. 'Godly,' she hissed.

'Godly?' the child repeated, smiling into Flora's anxious face. The densely embellished right sleeve raised itself as the girl lifted her arm. The small hand made a lyrical gesture up towards the heavens and back in an arc to the ground: a movement that described beauty and love falling upon human lovers below, uniting as it touched them – bringing together, inevitably, her life and Michael's without greed or insistence.

'Yes, yes,' she stammered again. She felt stunned. She knew that she had had her answer, whatever it was. It would take her some time to figure out exactly what it meant.

The child hadn't finished. 'You must rise above,' she said thoughtfully. 'You must ascend.'

'Transcend,' the chaperone corrected.

'Ascend,' the child repeated.

Flora nodded. She sighed and said, 'Thank you.' She started to get up. The chaperone came forward and, without touching, showed her the directions in which she should go. For a moment the woman blocked any further sight of the child. She indicated that Flora should move away, not try to catch another glimpse of the goddess, not to say thank you again; the interview was over.

She walked clumsily from the chamber and staggered a few times as she followed two priestesses back to the waiting-room. She bowed farewell to everyone. She let James take her by the arm. As they were ushered out, she leaned against him.

As soon as they passed outside the main gates, he began to hurry her along.

'Why are we going so fast?' she complained.

'Because you look terrible. I want to get you back into the car. You look like you're ready to faint again.'

'You're going too fast. I can't keep up.'

'Try, Flora,' he said. 'We can carry you if we have to.'

'No.'

'Christ knows why I let you talk me into this. What did she do – say she saw the ace of spades in your palm, or something? Jesus.' He and Michael bundled her into the car and they started on the drive to town.

She fell back in the seat. She still couldn't think clearly. *I must ascend*, she thought. It might be painful, but it would be necessary. *Did she mean that I have to rise above earthly love?* Maybe what the goddess had meant was that in the end everyone died and went to heaven, so it wasn't worth getting upset over unimportant things.

And perhaps the girl had also meant exactly what she'd said about love – that it was from heaven, freely given and necessary, but that rich people never had to feel necessity; if a friendship broke down, or a marriage, or a blood relationship, they somehow always managed to buy another one. Life could be made very agreeable that way. But love was what the goddess had said it was – not pure: poor.

'Well?' James asked.

'Better,' she said.

'Thank God for that. What did the creature do to you?'

'She told me I had to rise above.'

'Rise above what?'

'Oh, everything, I guess.'

'And that's what knocked you out – the Eastern version of moral uplift?'

'I just suddenly felt sort of . . . I don't know.'

He bent towards her, kissed her near her ear and whispered, 'Pregnant.'

'No.'

'Sure? You've been close to fainting twice.'

'Yes,' she said. 'Yes, I'm sure. No. What did you think of it all, Michael?'

'Very interesting indeed,' Michael answered. 'It's another way of life.'

'What did you think of her? The goddess.'

'Cute-looking little kid, but skinny as a rail underneath all those party clothes. You wonder if they feed them enough.'

'Those hundreds of people on litters believe she can cure them.'

'Yeah, well, they're sick. Sick people believe in anything.'

'Maybe they're right. Sometimes if you have faith, it makes things true.'

James groaned slightly with impatience.

Michael said, 'It's deception. Self-deception always makes people feel good. But it wouldn't fix a broken leg, if that's what was wrong with you. It might help you get better quicker, once a doctor's done the real work – see what I mean?'

'Yes, I see,' she said. He didn't understand. But there was no reason why he should. James said that she was tired and upset. 'We'll be back soon,' he assured her. 'And let's have an early lunch. I'm hungry as hell from getting up so early.'

'Is it still morning? You didn't think much of her, either, did you?'

'I thought she looked great, really fabulous – the dress, like a walking cyclamen plant, and the whole effect very pretty but a bit bizarre: like a gnome out of a fairy-tale. What I don't like is how she knocked the wind out of you. They aren't supposed to do that. They're supposed to give comfort and strength. That's the nature of the job.'

'She did. She gave me something to think about, anyway. All the rest of me was trying to get out what I wanted to say.'

He held her hand. He didn't ask what her request had been. He probably thought he knew; he'd think she'd have wanted to know something like, 'Why can't I be happy?' Everybody wanted happiness.

The car speeded up along the stretches by the coastline. They opened the windows and got a whiff of the sea before returning to air-conditioning. Flora breathed deeply. All beaches were the same: salt and iodine, like the summers of her childhood. New Caledonia would be like this, too.

They reached town before noon. James ordered the car to wait down a side street. The three of them got out and walked to one of the nice restaurants they had tried several times before. Flora was all right now, except that she felt bemused. She could walk without any trouble but she couldn't stop thinking about the temple and the goddess. She especially couldn't stop remembering the expression of joyful serenity on the child's face. It seemed to her that if she kept up the attempt to recapture the way it looked, she wouldn't have to let go of it.

The whole business had gone very quickly, as matters usually did when well organized, and paid for, in advance. And now they were having a good meal in a comfortable restaurant; and only at that moment did Flora recall that she'd meant to go up to Irma on her way out and hand her some money in an envelope.

'Eat,' James said.

She shook her head.

'Just a little,' he insisted.

She picked up the china spoon and looked at it. She put it into the soup bowl. James watched patiently. When the children had been small, he was always the one who could make them eat when they didn't want to, and later, make them brush their teeth: he let you know, without saying anything, that he was prepared to wait for ever, unchanging and with arms folded, until you did the right thing. Authority. And he never bothered with modern ideas about explaining things rationally. If the children asked, 'Why do I have to?' he'd answer, 'Because I say so.'

She began slowly, then ate hungrily. Before the coffee, she went off to the ladies' room for a long time and while she was there made sure that her face and hair looked perfect. She even thought of brushing her teeth with the travelling toothbrush she carried in her purse, but she'd be back at the hotel soon – she could do it there. James smiled approvingly as she emerged.

They sauntered out into the hot, dusty street again.

'Museum?' he suggested, 'or siesta?'

'A little nap might be nice. Is that all right with you, Michael?'

'Sure, fine,' Michael said.

James stopped on the corner. 'Where was that museum, anyhow?' he asked. 'Down around that street there somewhere, isn't it?'

Michael looked up. He began to point things out in the distance. Flora kept walking around the bend as the street curved to the right. She drew back against the buildings to avoid three boys who were standing together and talking in whispers. But as soon as she was clear, two others came out of a doorway. She started to move away, but they came straight towards her. And suddenly the first three, their friends, were behind her, snatching at her arms. It was the same as the day before, but this time she screamed loudly for Michael before the hands started to grip over her eyes and mouth. She also kicked and thrashed while they dragged her along the sidewalk. Right at the beginning, except for her own outburst, all the violent pushing and shoving took place to the accompaniment of low mutters and hisses. Only when James and Michael came charging around the corner did the real noise begin.

The gang had guns. The man now left alone to hold Flora from behind was jabbing something into her backbone. She knew it was a gun because she saw two of the others pull out pistols. They went for James. The voice behind her yelled, 'Stop, or we kill the woman.' Flora kept still, in case her struggling caused the weapon to go off by mistake. But Michael had his own gun in his hand and was crouched down in the road. He shot the two who were heading towards James, the third, who was waving a pistol in the air, and there was a fourth explosion landing someplace where Flora couldn't see. The arm around her gripped so tightly that she was suffocating. The voice, sounding deranged, screamed into her ear, 'You drop the gun, or I kill her!' She knew he meant it. He'd do anything. He might even kill her without knowing what he was doing.

Michael didn't hesitate. She saw him turn towards them and the look on his face was nothing: it was like being confronted by a machine. He fired right at her. She should have known.

She didn't fall straight away. The man who had held her lay dead on the ground while she swayed above him. She knew she'd been shot, but not where. It felt as if she'd been hit by a truck. And suddenly she saw that there was blood everywhere – maybe hers, maybe other people's.

She should have known that a man formed by the conventions of the world into which she had married would already have his loyalties arranged in order of importance, and that the men and male heirs to the line would always take precedence over the outsiders who had fitted themselves into their lives. James was central; she was only decoration. As long as one man in the street was left with a gun, that was a danger to James. In Michael's eyes she had passed during less than three minutes from object to obstacle. He'd shot her to pieces, and, using her as a target, killed the gunman behind her.

James had his arms around her. He was calling out for an ambulance. There were plenty of other people on the street now. And she thought: *My God, how embarrassing: I've wet my pants.*

But what she said was, 'I'm bleeding,' and passed out.

She woke up looking at a wall, at window-blinds, at the ceiling. Everything hurt.

It was still daylight, so perhaps she hadn't been there very long. Or maybe it was the next day. It felt like a long time. She was trussed like a swaddled baby and she was hooked up to a lot of tubes – she could see that, too. And she was terrified that parts of her body had been shattered beyond repair: that they would be crippled so badly that they'd never move again, that perhaps the doctors had amputated limbs. The fear was even worse than the pain.

Someone got up from behind all the machinery on her other side and left the room.

James came from around the back of her bed and sat in a chair next to her. He looked tired. And sad, too. That was unusual; she'd hardly ever seen him looking sad. He reached over and put his hand on her bare right arm, which lay outside the covers. She realized that she must be naked underneath; only bandages, no nightgown.

'You're going to be all right,' he told her.

She believed him. She said, 'Hurts a lot.' He smiled grimly. She asked, 'How long have I been here?'

'Twenty-four hours.'

'You haven't shaved.'

He kept squeezing her arm lightly and looking into her face. She thought she was about to go back to sleep again, but he caught her attention by saying her name.

'Would you do something for me?'

She said, 'Of course. You're always so good to me.'

He put his head down on the bed for a while and sighed. He really did love her, she thought, but she'd never believed it before.

'If you could talk to Michael,' he said. 'Just a couple of seconds. He feels so broken up about how it happened. If you could just let him know you understand.'

'I understand,' she said.

'I mean, tell him you forgive him. He hasn't said much, but he hasn't been able to eat or sleep, either. Or shave. Can I tell him to come in?'

She suddenly sensed that everything was draining away from

her, never to return. She tried to hold on, but it was no use.

'Flora?'

The horror passed. She felt better. The fear had left, along with all the rest. She knew that she was going to die.

'Yes,' she said. 'Tell him to come in.'

James went away. She heard his footsteps. And Michael's; heard James saying, 'Just a couple of seconds. She's very tired,' and saw him moving away out of the room as Michael sat down in the chair. She turned her head to look at him.

He was smiling. Even with her head to the side, she could see his expression exactly: a nasty little smile. His drunken uncle had been chauffeur and pander to the old man and his cousins; and, of course, Michael would have taken over the same office for the sons. She should have known. It was that kind of family: even the employees were inheritable.

Everything was obvious now, and especially the fact that Michael's unshakeable politeness and deference had been an indication of his distaste for her. He'd given up pretending, now that he knew she was dying. It was more than distaste. It must be a real hatred, because he couldn't help it any longer. He wanted to show her, even with James just outside the door.

'I want you to understand,' he said quietly.

'No need,' she answered.

'You got to understand, it's for him. Far as I'm concerned, I don't give a shit. You've just got to tell him you forgive me. Then it'll be okay.'

Everything would be all right. It was simple, if you had that much money. When they reported the attack, James would see to it that everyone thought she'd been shot by the kidnappers, not by Michael. Who would question it? Two respectable witnesses; and dead men who were known criminals. The hospital would get a new wing, the police force a large donation. It would be easy. It would have been easy even if they'd deliberately set out to murder her and hired the men to do it.

'If it was me,' Michael said, leaning forward, 'I'd be counting the minutes till you go down the tubes. "Oh James dear, look at that, oh isn't that perfectly sweet? Can I have the car window open, if it's all right with Michael: can I have it closed, if Michael doesn't mind?" Pain in the ass is what you are. I mean, I seen plenty: one to a hundred I used to mark them, and you rate down around ten, sweetheart. A real lemon. "Am I doing this right, am I doing that?" I told him, "Jimbo, this one's a dud." And he just said, "No, Kelvin, this time I'm choosing for myself." He wouldn't listen.'

James could do it right next time, she thought. He'd marry again, perhaps quite soon, and be just as content. He'd probably go to New Caledonia after all, maybe with another woman, or just with Michael. Someone else would bring up her children, no doubt doing it very well. They'd have the photographs of her, so everyone could remember how pretty she'd been; she had always taken a good picture. The family would be able to choose the new wife, as they'd chosen for Edward. She'd been crazy about Edward; that was how everything had started. It was enough to make you laugh. But she had to stop thinking about it. She had to ascend. All the events in the house and all the holiday travelling would still go on, only she wouldn't be able to have any part in them. She had to rise above.

'I forgive,' she said. It was becoming difficult for her to speak.

'I'll get him,' Michael told her. He stood up.

'Wait.' She started to breathe quickly.

He leaned across the bed to look at her face. He said, 'I'll get somebody.'

'Michael,' she said clearly, 'I loved you.'

He stepped back. The smile vanished. He looked revolted, infuriated.

'I loved you,' she repeated. 'With all my heart.' Her lips curved together, her eyes closed, her head moved to the side. She was gone.

Michael began to scream.

The sound brought James running into the room, and two nurses after him.

Michael caught Flora up in his arms. He shouted into her closed face. He tried to slam her against the wall. James pulled him back. 'It's all right,' he said. 'Stop.'

'Bitch,' Michael yelled at Flora. 'Take it back. Take it back, you lousy bitch.'

'Calm down,' James said. 'She forgives you.' He got his arm around both of them and tugged. Michael let go, dropping Flora's body. She fell face downward. The nurses stooped to pick her up from the floor.

James and Michael stood grappled together, their faces wet with tears and sweat. Michael stared at the wall in front of him.

'It's all right,' James told him. 'She understands. Don't worry. After people die, they understand everything.'

Inheritance

When Carla's marriage broke up, everyone from her father's branch of the family felt obliged to load her with so much pity and advice that she didn't think she'd be able to last out the summer with them. Sometimes their kindness made her feel even worse: her Aunt Grace, for instance, had laid a hand on her arm and told her not to mind: time would heal the wound, and besides, think of how much worse it could have been – she might have had children.

When her grandmother died, that put the lid on it. She'd loved her grandmother. They'd always been able to talk together, rattling along like schoolfriends. In the last months of her life, her grandmother had done several things that other people considered eccentric, or even crazy. Carla knew better, because the old woman had explained to her beforehand: she'd said, 'It may not come now, but if it does, I want to be prepared. I don't like leaving things in a mess. And legal formalities can be intimidating to simple people – to the kind of people who live around here.' She was referring to old acquaintances; they included the cook, maid and handyman who had worked in and around the house over the past fifty years. She'd left most of them something in her will, but in addition she wanted them to have mementoes that wouldn't be taxable to the estate or come to them through the lawyers. She spent a lot of time on the phone, arranging for certain items of furniture to be collected and driven to the houses of friends. She sent cash through the mail – something everyone, even people not related to her, knew was crazy – and had it arrive safely.

Finally, one day, she asked Carla to get all the jewellers' boxes and silk pouches out of the safe. And she'd proceeded to put on every necklace, bracelet, pin and ring that she owned.

'Which ones do you like best?' she'd asked.

'The lizard pin,' Carla had said, 'and the gold link bracelet, and the ring with the tiny rubies – that's always been my favourite.'

'It's not valuable. Very ordinary stones.'

'I love it.'

Her grandmother had put the brooch and bracelet into her hand and slid the ring on to her finger – the same finger on which Carla had worn her wedding ring.

'And it fits,' Carla had said.

'Stop Minnie from being so scandalized. If you don't want to wear your wedding ring any longer, there's no reason why you should.'

'I wouldn't want to. But even if I did, I couldn't. It broke. It broke in pieces on the day he walked out. I just put my hand up on the edge of the sink when I was reaching down to get my heavy frying pan out of the cupboard, just as usual, and the ring fell into separate pieces. There must have been a fault in the metal. It upset me so much – more than almost anything else. The exact same day: can you imagine? It's enough to make you believe – I don't know.'

'Yes, there's no doubt these things happen. Nobody can explain them. I remember when Father was in the hospital; we were sitting together, waiting for news, and all at once there was a loud crash from the library: his portrait had fallen off the wall. Maybe you've guessed – we had the news shortly afterwards that he'd died, and it must have been at that very moment.' She picked out several other small pieces of jewellery to present to Carla. 'Promise me', she said, 'you'll wear them or you'll give them away to somebody else who'll wear them. What I don't want you to do is to put everything in a drawer somewhere and save it. It's the same with life, the same with love. You've got to use it, enjoy it – be happy with it. And if you lose it, so be it: never mind.'

'Oh, I'll wear them,' Carla promised.

'It took me a long time to learn that,' her grandmother added. 'It was a conclusion I came to really rather late.'

They got into the old Plymouth – the only car her grandmother still trusted – and Carla drove from one house to another. She'd stop the car, help the old woman out and then stand aside as the friend, ex-servant or acquaintance was asked, 'Which one do you like best?' As soon as the object had been handed over, her grandmother said that she had several calls to make and had to be going. Carla noticed that a nice etiquette was observed: towards the end of the day, the recipients were not asked to choose. Her grandmother would simply pluck some jewel from its place and say, 'I wanted you to have this.'

A few weeks later, she died. No pictures fell from the wall, nor were there other portents. Carla was desolate. The aunts and uncles started to divide up the furniture. She received instructions from her cousins about how to hang on to their share, too. Her father flew in for the funeral, but his wife didn't bother to attend. He looked and obviously felt uncomfortable, trying to give correct formal expression to feelings he hadn't possessed.

Carla felt sorry for him. They went for a walk through the woods on the trail starting from where the old stables had been. He asked her about her plans for the future.

'Go back to my job, I guess. I don't want to. I don't want to be in the same town with him. I'd like to make a complete break with everything, just go away somewhere. I really would.'

'You could come stay with us,' he told her. She was touched.

'In a year, maybe,' she said. 'I'd love to. I'll have to get things organized, think about money.'

'Oh, I'm sure we could get you the ticket. And Marsha would love it.'

Marsha wouldn't love it; she'd hate every minute, but she'd have to lump it. For a moment Carla thought she might take up the offer. She liked the idea, she said, but she wanted to wait a while.

Her grandmother had left her some money and a few stocks and shares, which she could either save or use immediately. If she dropped everything and just went wandering around the world, she could probably last for three years. And in the meantime, the business she'd built up over the past five years would fall apart.

She was a designer. She'd started out with the idea that she'd go into textiles and end up with her own range of fabrics and clothes. But she hadn't been able to fight her way into the profession. She'd done a few magazine ads and cartoons for the newspapers, and got her first good assignment through a friend: illustrating birthday cards. That had led to the Kassels, who ran a toyshop that stocked the cards. From her first week with them she was designing the toys and overseeing their manufacture, and getting the coffee and sandwiches ready in the back room while first Mrs Kassel and then Mr Kassel came to her for advice: crying, telling her that the family was breaking up and their lives were over and why hadn't they had a daughter like her. The business was booming, thanks to Carla – or, rather, thanks to her work and the Kassels' ability to push it towards customers with all the enthusiasm they felt for it; she could never have done that by herself. The business continued to prosper while the family did in fact split and Carla had to take sides. And her husband began to feel that she wasn't paying enough attention to him. It was still doing all right when she set up on her own and it was her turn to cry all over both the Kassels about her husband.

And now her own business was a success, expanding all the time. She could send in work while someone else held the fort for her. But not for three years. Three months, maybe. She thought hard about where she could go for three months only. And suddenly she remembered the other side of the family: her mother's side. There was a little gang of great-aunts still living up in what had been her mother's home town. They'd all be pretty old now. She thought she ought to see them.

She told her father the next morning, the day of his flight out, that she'd decided to use the next couple of months looking up her mother's relatives. 'I've forgotten the name of the town they live in, though.'

He told her the name and wrote it down. He even remembered the right street. 'They're rather strange people,' he warned her. 'I thought so when I met them. Half of them can't even speak English.'

'That's all right. And maybe we won't like each other, but I just feel that we should try; that I ought to get to know them before it's too late.' She didn't say that – beginning with the break-up of her parents' marriage – she had started to fear the weakening of any family ties. Her fear might even have contributed to the ending of her own marriage. Families should stick together, she believed.

When she left her grandmother's house, the others were already busy with their own affairs and hardly noticed her departure. Two of her aunts had stopped speaking to each other because of what her father referred to as a 'misunderstanding'. But there had been no failure to understand. The two women both wanted the same thing, that was all: they were fighting

over who was to get the Chinese jade buffalo. Carla was glad
that her grandmother had given her the special pieces of jewellery outright, with her own hands, on that day of presentations.
Twice during the plane flight up north she stopped reading her
book, held her hand up and turned it to the side so that the light
from the small airplane window shone over the bracelet and
ring. She could remember them both from all the way back to
the beginning of her childhood.

The part of town where her great-aunts lived was a place of
broad avenues, green lawns and big trees. The houses too were
very large and decorated with bannistered porches, balconies
and verandahs. The district definitely didn't look like one
where you'd find people who, as her father had told her, could
barely speak English. Nor had the letter she'd received read like
the work of an illiterate. On the contrary, the language had been
precise – in fact, almost stilted, although grammatically fault-
less.

She lost her way among the peculiar numbering systems of
the neighbourhood. As she was beginning to feel tired enough
to risk the embarrassment of ringing a doorbell and asking for
directions, she saw a mailman turn the corner and come towards
her. He was a grey-haired man who looked as if he'd had the
job for many years and knew all about the city. When she asked
him, indicating her useless map, he said, 'Oh, the Countess.
Sure.'

'Countess?'

'That's what she calls herself.'

There was no way of telling if the man thought her great-aunt
was pretentious, silly, or actually out of her mind. He told Carla
that she'd missed one of the turns and was in exactly the right
spot on a parallel street.

'Just one block away,' he said, pointing. Then it was easy. She
was held up only a few more minutes, and that was because she
couldn't believe that the house with the number was the one
she was looking for; it was about the size of a nice old country
hotel.

She walked down the path, up the stairs to the porch, and
rang the bell. The front door stood open, only the screen door
was shut. Through it she could see a hallway, a table with
flowers, the foot of a magnificent stairway; and an old woman

tottering towards her, a uniformed maid at her elbow. The maid reached the screen door first and opened it. Carla stepped forward.

The old woman held out her arms. 'At last,' she crooned. 'My dear little Carla. Oh, what a joy – oh, if only your mother were alive at this moment.'

Carla allowed herself to be embraced, and she kissed the great-aunt on both cheeks. She also realized that she'd been led astray by what could genuinely have been described as a misunderstanding: there was nothing wrong with her aunt's education or upbringing – it was just that she spoke a different language. She was speaking German.

'Well,' the aunt said. 'Yes, lovely. Did your mother bring you up to understand German?'

Carla said, 'No, she wasn't – I was with my grandparents most of the time.'

'Of course,' the old woman said, switching to English. 'We tried to make them allow you to stay up here with us. But they wouldn't.'

'I learned French and German in high school.'

'Yes?'

'And I kept it up in college when I was bumming around Europe in the summer—'

The old woman lapsed into German again, asking questions.

'But I've forgotten a lot,' Carla went on. 'And I'm pretty slow. I was always stumbling around, even at my best. My accent was OK, but I never got the genders right. And that stuff about matching up the adjectives in the dative – well, I sort of skipped that side of it.'

'We'll have to do something about that. But not today – no, there's no need to be nervous. Now, where is your suitcase?'

'At the motel.'

'We'll have it brought. You'll stay here, naturally. I'm your Aunt Gisela, by the way.'

'You wrote the letter.'

'I wrote it. The others didn't want to answer. Ridiculous. Come in here and we'll have some coffee and I'll tell you about it.' She led Carla through a wide hallway, across oriental rugs, past furniture polished until it shimmered. In a far corner of the room where they sat down a grand piano gleamed as if made of patent leather.

The maid reappeared without having been summoned.

'Bring us some coffee, Agnes,' Aunt Gisela said. 'And the usual . . . sandwiches and cakes.'

'Crackers?'

'Cupcakes. *Kuchen.*' When Agnes had gone, she said, 'That's the one I still mix up. And she gets so angry if I want to send them back to the kitchen.'

'This is a wonderful house,' Carla said.

'Quite nice, yes. We had better in Germany. We had palaces.'

'Really?'

'Didn't your mother tell you anything?'

'I was only ten when she died. I can't remember that she ever talked about her family at all, not once.'

Aunt Gisela sat forward in her chair. She told Carla that she had come from an ancient, important and persecuted aristocratic family and that quite aside from the significance of being heir to a rich cultural heritage, there was the question of the actual property. Some of the buildings and estates were unavailable at the moment: they lay in Poland, East Germany and Lithuania. But there were others.

'One doesn't want things to go out of the family,' she said. 'Of course, it's important to have museums, but it's better that all those objects should be in daily use.'

Carla shifted her attention as Agnes brought the coffee. Her aunt said, 'Would you mind pouring? My hand is still steady, but sometimes I pour a perfect cup just half an inch beyond where it should be. All over the table, over the floor.'

Carla poured out the coffee and busied herself with the plates. She said, 'My other great-aunts—'

'Gerda and Ursula. You'll have to discount everything they say. They're old-fashioned and absurd. There are so few young ones in the great families nowadays. We have to forgive and forget.'

'That's what I think,' Carla said. 'Especially now. I wrote you: my grandmother just died. I think we should get together and be friends while we can. When people die, it's too late. But I wouldn't want to stay here in the house if they don't want me.'

'You are my guest,' Gisela said. In four bites she made a neat meal of one of the small iced cupcakes. She lifted her hand to the plate again. Her movements were exceptionally light and quick for a woman of her age. And she was extraordinarily thin for someone who was in the habit of gobbling cakes. Carla herself stopped at one and refused a second sandwich. She gave her attention to the family history: where they had all lived, how many houses and castles they'd owned, how many wars they'd been through.

'There aren't many of us left,' Aunt Gisela said. She raised her coffee cup and added, 'As you say: we can't afford to keep up family quarrels.'

Carla smiled, but she suddenly felt less welcome. She was glad that for the first night at least she'd be in the motel.

After their coffee, she was shown around the gardens at the other side of the house. They were bordered by four noble trees and were full of flowerbeds. The beds were laid out in an orderly way that made the whole of the back yard appear clean and regimented.

'This must take a lot of work,' Carla commented.

Her aunt nodded and said complacently, yes.

A little later, as the afternoon light was beginning to soften, she met the other two aunts: Gerda and Ursula. Ursula was tall, thin, dignified and not very talkative. Gerda was bunchily plump, had scanty brown hair, and stared at Carla, leaning close; in both of her eyes the iris was ringed in white. Carla wasn't sure what that meant, other than that it was something you often noticed in old people's eyes. It might just be a sign of age, not of disease or partial blindness.

'I see you're wearing the lizard pin,' Gerda said. Her eyesight was good enough for that, at least.

'My grandmother's.'

'I know. I remember. I have a photographic memory for jewels. If we'd been the right age, or from the kind of family that went into trade, I should have been connected with a jewellery business. Yes, definitely – I have a feeling for it, despite the unfortunate family failing. You too? You find yourself drawn to shiny objects and colour?'

'Not specially. I just have this strong sentimental attachment for the things I saw my grandmother wearing when I was a little girl.'

They sat down on the side of the room near the piano. Ursula began to play. She took every piece very slowly. Carla was invited to replace her at the keyboard; she had to explain that she'd never learned more than a few short works, had been bored by her music teacher, still couldn't read the bottom clef, and had begged to give up after a year.

'How you must regret it now,' Gisela said.

'Not at all. It was completely wasted time. I never had any talent for playing. I like listening.'

'One wouldn't expect you to be a Paderewski, dear. It's simply a necessary accomplishment.'

'I don't', Carla said, 'find it necessary.'

'Ah,' Gisela murmured.

Disapproval seemed to radiate towards her from all three women. She wanted to get up and go back to her motel and rest for a couple of hours. She'd almost reached the end of her time-limit for chat with strangers. Having to do part of it in German was an added strain. 'What's the family failing?' she asked.

'We're pearlkillers,' Gerda said.

'What's that?'

'Did you know that there were such people?'

'No.' She still had no idea what the phrase meant, either in English or in German.

'That's right,' Gisela said. 'It's true. Something to do with the chemicals in the skin.'

'Oh?'

'But I don't think little Carla is interested in hearing about that kind of thing.'

'Well, she should be,' Gerda said. 'It's a family characteristic. Did your grandmother ever wear pearls, Carla?'

'Yes, she had a long rope with knots between the pearls in case the string broke. She wore them all the time. One of my aunts has them now.'

'She wore them all the time because you have to. Pearls need to be kept in touch with the oils of the skin in order to retain their lustre. They can dry out if you keep them in a box.'

'There are some people', Gisela said, 'who have a theory that you should also wear them when you swim in the ocean – to return them to their home – but I can't believe the salt would be good for them.'

'Most of the ladies we used to know', Gerda continued, 'had pearls. And when they weren't wearing them, they made the maids wear them, to keep the pearls healthy. The younger the skin, the better it was supposed to be. But there are some people whose skin produces a chemical harmful to pearls – if they wear a ring for a while, suddenly they'll notice that the pearls have shrunk and almost withered back into the setting.'

'Pearlkillers,' Gisela said. 'Our whole family. You may be one, too. We had an aunt who didn't develop the symptoms till late in life; then she let one of the maids wear her pearls while she tried to find a buyer for them, and – guess what? The maid turned out to be a pearlkiller, too. We thought that was extremely funny.'

'And very suspicious,' Gerda added. 'Sometimes servants acquire the family traits out of affectation or a desire to emulate. But to be a pearlkiller presupposes an inherited tendency. Doesn't it?'

'I don't know,' Carla said. 'She might have had a family with the same kind of thing.'

'Servants don't have families. They're parasitic in that respect. They want the family they're working for. They love them and they hate and envy them. It's like biographers and the famous. What I could tell you about servants.'

'Has Agnes been with you long?'

'Agnes. That slut. A real camel.'

Gisela said quietly, 'We've had a certain amount of trouble with Agnes.'

'Oh?'

'She's been going out with some much younger man,' Gerda said. 'A fortune-hunter. He thinks we'd leave her our money. As if we would.'

'He must be half her age,' Gisela said. 'There can't be anything in it.'

'Don't deceive yourself. Agnes does it with anyone. She drinks like a fish, and then she doesn't care who it is. Yes, it's true. She goes to bars and picks up men and they go somewhere together. Some hotel that specializes in that kind of thing, I suppose.'

'We have no way of knowing that,' Gisela told her.

'Some of these old families, you know,' Gerda muttered; 'the servants even look a lot like the masters.'

'That could be psychological,' Carla said. 'Or psychosomatic.'

'Yes. There's also a word for family relationships that become substitutional.'

'What?' Gisela said.

'Subst—'

'Yes, I heard it. I just don't know what it means.'

'Ah. Let's say: the brother in a family commits a crime. He'd be punished, but then so would the other members – his parents and sister, and so on. They wouldn't be precisely what you could call guilty, but they'd be associated by virtue of their kinship. There would be a group liability. In German that would be called *Sippenhaft*. You understand?'

Carla said, 'Sure – it's so they won't be able to take revenge for the brother being punished.'

'I assume that's what's behind it.'

'Primitive.'

'And effective,' Gerda said. 'The cruel methods primitive peoples have of dealing with disease – they prevent it from spreading. There are other plagues, too, and epidemics. There are evil ideas, for instance.'

Carla sighed. The muscles in her neck and shoulders ached from having to sit at attention. She thought of saying that the methods of primitive peoples hadn't saved them from being wiped out by measles and the common cold; but that would simply lead Aunt Gerda to some new topic. Did they always talk like that – jumping all over the place and never letting up? Or was it just because she was a new face? She said, 'You know, I think I'd like to go back to the motel to rest for a little. I'm kind of tired out from the trip.'

'Oh, you can't go till after supper,' Gisela pleaded.

'Let her go,' Gerda said.

At the piano Ursula stopped playing. She lifted both hands from the keyboard in a concert-hall flourish. She looked at Carla. 'Your mother', she told her, 'betrayed her family.'

'She married an outsider, that's all.'

'We always marry Germans.'

'Or if you don't, you don't get married?'

'That's right. It's better than ending the way she did.'

Carla stood up. Gisela, slowly, tried to follow; she scolded Ursula for her tactlessness.

Carla moved quickly from the room. Behind her she heard the piano starting again. Ahead of her Agnes – large-nosed, thin-lipped, with her hair scraped into a bun and a smirk on her face – reached for the screen door.

'Carla dear, please wait,' Gisela begged.

As the old woman came wheezing up to her, Carla turned and

held out her hands. 'Aunt Gisela, it's been really nice meeting you,' she said, 'but not the others.'

'They don't understand. They don't see anybody all year long. They forget how to behave. I'm the one who deals with everything. They haven't been out of the house and garden for over twenty years. I think your mother's engagement party was the last time they went out. And that was only to make a big scene and say they wouldn't come to the wedding. You have to understand. They're old.'

'Were they wonderful and kind when they were younger?'

'Well, I suppose they've always been difficult.'

'I'll see you tomorrow,' Carla said.

'Yes, please. Please, Carla. I want to ask a great favour of you. There's something I want you to get for us. My cousin, Theo, took it. It didn't belong to him – it belongs to us. You will promise, won't you?'

'I'll come see you tomorrow,' she said. 'I've got to go now.' Agnes swung the door ahead of her.

She ran down the steps and away.

She lay on the bed in her motel room and wondered if she'd have the nerve to pack up and just get out in the morning, leaving one of those messages that said, 'Called away suddenly'. But that was what other people had done to her all her life; she couldn't be the one to do it to someone else. She especially shouldn't do it to Aunt Gisela, who didn't deserve to be treated like that. Aunt Gerda would be a different matter. And the other one, Ursula: sane but nasty.

She also wished that she had a very large drink. She should have bought a bottle someplace. She wasn't the kind of woman who went into bars on her own. She didn't really want to go swimming alone in the motel pool, either, but if she just stayed sitting in her room, she might start thinking about her ex-husband again. She might even imagine how her divorced mother had felt after she'd left her child with its grandparents. Her mother had checked into a motel room – maybe a room very similar to that one: and had ended up cutting her wrists.

The view from the windows showed a parking lot and beyond it the old jetties. Across the river stood abandoned brick ware-houses and behind them, pine trees. The sky was a firm, northern blue, only just beginning to darken. Even in her aunts' neighbourhood, among the large houses and plush green lawns, the sky had that look. It reminded you that nearby were the lakes as big as seas, and the unbroken miles of evergreen forest that used to be the country of the Indians.

Her telephone rang. When she picked it up a man's voice told her that he'd had a call from her great-aunt Gisela and he'd like to talk to her for a few minutes, in person, if she didn't mind. His name was Carl Raymond.

'That sounds like two people,' she said.

'What?'

'When did you want to meet?'

'I kind of thought right now. I could take you out for supper and we could talk. My uncle George is your aunts' accountant.'

'Oh,' she said. The information meant nothing, if true, but it persuaded her.

She took a shower and changed into a dress that was still slightly wrinkled over the skirt.

He was waiting at the reception desk. He'd been gossiping and joking with the clerk, who said to her, 'I didn't know you were a friend of Carl here, Miss.'

'We've never met,' she said. She put the key down on the counter and held out her hand; Carl shook it. He said he was glad to meet her: they had a lot to talk about. 'First of all, some food.'

'What's wrong with here?' the clerk asked.

'Go on,' Carl said. He took her by the elbow and led her out to a car. He told her, 'It's a long story, and I've just come off work. I'm going to need a drink before I can get it straightened out.'

'That's fine by me,' she said. She began to perk up. Always, she thought, just when she was ready to throw in the towel, something nice turned up. And she still hadn't learned that it always would: the pleasant and unpleasant ran in tandem. But whenever she began to feel dejected, she forgot: the bad times seemed to be going on for ever. Maybe it was possible that she'd inherited the predilection from her mother.

He parked the car and took her in to the kind of bar and grill that made the customers put on ties. The lighting was subdued enough to hide her badly-ironed skirt.

They each had two drinks. She got a good look at him while he was ordering the meal: he was tall and well-built, about her own age and had a squarish head, pale blue eyes, a strong-featured face, small regular teeth. His hair was straight and light, clipped short – almost like a crew cut, which made his ears appear to stick out a little. Most people would have considered him a good-looking man. She thought he was all right: nice but rather uninteresting. She'd grown too used to her husband's dark, frizzy-haired, ugly-romantic looks.

'Carl and Carla,' he said. 'That's sort of a coincidence, isn't it?'

'That's right. We sound like a comedy team.'

'Well, some kind of a team, anyway. I'll drink to that.'

'So you're an accountant?' she said.

'No, I'm in real estate. It's my uncle George who's their accountant. At least, he's still your aunt – your great-aunt – Gisela's, but there've been arguments with the other two. Maybe you didn't know it, but your aunts have a big reputation in this neck of the woods for—'

'Eccentricity?'

'And general cussedness. And when they don't have much to occupy their time with, they get on the phone and try to strike points against each other through a third person.'

'Uncle George.'

'And Uncle Bertram at the bank and my father, before he picked up and moved. He was in the same firm as one of their lawyers, Sandy Howe. Mr Howe used to say it was a lean week when one of them didn't want to change her will. Anyway, I guess they're an institution by now. Life wouldn't be so colourful without them. And they went through quite a lot during the war; during both wars, there was a lot of anti-German feeling.'

'But they've lived here for a hundred years.'

'They didn't mix. They wouldn't talk English. They wouldn't marry anybody who wasn't from a German background. My family was mostly German, too. A lot of this town was. But nobody else thinks of it that way. We're all American. Your aunts aren't. They never wanted to be. And they told everybody about their titles.'

'That wouldn't have made them disliked. That's something everybody laughs at. Even the mailmen.'

'It isn't democratic.'

'If it's true.'

'Oh, it's certainly true.'

'Really?'

'Without a doubt.' He began to tell her about the family's holdings in Eastern Europe.

Their food came and he continued to talk. She could see he

was a man who could be driven to frenzy by the idea of large stretches of saleable land. She wondered if perhaps the three old women had decided to bamboozle him just for fun.

Over coffee he went on to tell her about the houses and estates they still had in countries that recognized their ownership. 'They're millionaires,' he said. 'Multi-millionaires.'

'Nice.'

'I just wanted you to know that if there's any difficulty about the estate, you could fight it.'

'What do you mean?'

'You're the heir, aren't you?'

'No.'

'Surely.'

'Not at all. They cut my mother right out of their lives when she married.'

'Your mother, but not you.'

'Me too, I'm sure. It's what they call *Sippenhaft*.'

'I think you're the heir. And if you weren't, you could claim it. You could certainly claim it against the parlourmaid.'

'Agnes? What's she got to do with it?'

'She's one of the ones who's put into the wills and taken out again every week. It's how they keep her there. They make a promise and then they fight and they break it, and so on.'

'What a life. How can she stand it?'

'Not much choice, I guess.'

'But how can she believe it? Obviously it's a game they play.'

'Nope. If they sign all the right stuff, it's real. It's binding. You could try to prove afterwards that the way they kept changing their minds was a sign of mental decay, and that they were being taken advantage of; but you'd have to fight it through the courts. You couldn't just throw it out.'

'Well, it's no stranger than anything else. I don't think it has anything to do with me. But thanks for the information.'

'Right,' he said. 'Just thought you ought to know.'

He took her back to the motel, walked her to her room, waited till she'd unlocked the door, and then pulled her back and kissed her on the mouth before saying goodnight. She went inside, shut the door and stayed looking at it. It was too short an acquaintance for him to be kissing her. And it was a long time since anything like it had happened to her.

* * *

As she was getting ready to go in to breakfast, her phone rang. Aunt Gisela was on the line. She sounded a lot more quavery than Carla remembered.

'Please, dear, I know it must have been upsetting yesterday, but I'm not feeling very well – I don't have the time to smooth things over the way I used to. Would you come over, please?'

'All right,' Carla said. 'After I've had my breakfast. But just you. Not the others.'

'They're very sorry.'

'I doubt it.'

'What's that?'

'I said I don't believe it. Ursula did the dirty work and Gerda thought it was a scream. They got a lot of pleasure out of hurting me. And I'm not letting myself in for a second dose.'

'Oh, no. I'm sure—'

'I mean it. If I see them, I'm walking out again. Agreed?'

'Yes, dear,' Aunt Gisela said.

Carla felt that she had taken action and made everything clear. Before the divorce she'd never spoken harshly or even decisively to anyone. She ate a large breakfast. Over her last cup of coffee she remembered that the evening before, she'd been ready to get out altogether. Now she really didn't know what she was going to do except that when Carl had kissed her at the door she'd been given the impression of having a lover again. She could even have asked him in. It all started so easily, she thought. Again. She'd been sure she never wanted anything else to happen ever again.

Aunt Gisela arrived panting in the front hall. She hadn't been quick enough for Agnes, who whipped the screen door open and afterwards deliberately slammed it so that it twanged like a harp.

'The humidity today,' the old woman said, her breath whiffling; 'or perhaps the pollen.' She drew Carla down a side corridor and into a pleasant study overlooking part of the garden.

'This used to be Albert's room,' she said. She waved her hand at a leather armchair large enough to have been the favourite reading-chair of a fairly big man. Carla sat down in it.

Gisela seated herself bolt upright in a straight-backed

wooden chair. 'I must tell you some more about the family,' she said.

Carla leaned forward. Her aunt's narrative came out without pause, partly in English, partly in German, both broken by laboured breathing and a whistling from the lungs. Carla didn't dare interrupt. It seemed like the kind of speech people gave when about to be executed – it appeared to cover everything Gisela had ever thought or remembered about the family, and included statements to the effect that: they were all under a blight; they had done many great wrongs to several other large and important families hundreds of years ago; they had lost kingdoms, or places as good as kingdoms; they were of royal blood; some of the family, led by cousin Theo, had managed to swindle the others out of a very great deal of money and property and were living it up on their ranches in South America; Theo had absconded with something called 'Count Walter's Treasure', but it belonged to her – Gisela; he had ruined her when she was a girl and then laughed at her, and if there had been any consequences, she'd have had to – well, Carla knew what she'd have had to do. 'And now getting old,' she sighed. 'But if you get the Treasure back, Count Walter's, I'll be well again. And it's yours after me, you know. A part of your German inheritance.'

'I'll try,' Cárla said. The old woman was in such distress that she'd have promised almost anything to calm her down.

'I'll pay all expenses, naturally. Carl is seeing about the tickets now. And he's agreed to chaperone you. It wouldn't be right for you to go alone.'

'Where?'

'He'll be in Germany at this season. Or possibly in one of his Italian villas.'

'But—'

'Then it's all arranged. I'm so glad.'

'Aunt Gisela, I don't understand.'

'Priceless. I'll be well again when you've got it.'

'I don't even have my passport with me.'

'You remember the number?'

'Yes.'

'Good. We'll be able to do something.'

'How? That kind of thing takes time. And doesn't Carl have a job someplace?'

He's saved up a lot of vacation-time. You don't understand about Theo. Soon it's going to be too late. I'm too old now. We've got to have it.'

'Why?'

'If we die without the treasure . . . .'

'Yes?'

'I don't want to tell you.'

'When you say it's going to make you well: how's it going to do that?'

'By touch.'

'Is it a kind of relic or something?'

'Exactly. That's the word. Isn't it stupid – when I forget a word nowadays, I lose it from both languages. Occasionally I can get it again through the French or Italian. The mind is so weak, Carla. When you start wearing out.'

'And Carl would go, too?'

'He handles a lot of our business affairs now.'

'What happened to his father?'

'I believe they call it "mid-life crisis". He started to want young girls instead of his family.'

'Is Carl the only one?'

'There's another boy and a girl.'

'And their mother?'

'She's still here, complaining. You can see why he went. But she wasn't like that before he left. She's become a different person.'

Something made of metal clanked on to the floor just outside the door. It sounded like a bunch of keys. Aunt Gisela rose with an easy smoothness surprising in her condition. She opened the door.

Agnes stood outside, not looking in any way bothered; she said, 'Are you going to want lunch or what?'

'A light luncheon for two, Agnes. In here. And then you may leave us.'

'OK,' Agnes said. She slouched away.

Carla was on her feet, protesting that she had to go, she had to make phone calls about her business, she certainly couldn't spend more than a week on vacation.

Gisela over-ruled her. She said quietly, 'Yes, dear, yes,' patted her hand, smiled charmingly and added, 'but you know that I'm the one who really doesn't have time. I can see it running out as

clearly as if it were sand in an hour-glass. Just this one thing for
your old aunt, little Carla.'

The phone woke her up early. She'd swum back and forth in the
motel pool for twenty minutes the evening before, had had a
large drink with her salad-bar meal and slept like a log. They
weren't supposed to give her a morning call; she had an alarm
clock with her. It was still almost dark.

'Yes?' she said into the receiver.

'It's Carl. I've got some bad news.'

She thought something must have happened to Gisela – a
stroke or collapse of some kind. Or, maybe after all the excitement of the day and the amount of talking she'd done, actually
her death.

'Didn't you hear the sirens?' he asked.

'What?'

At some time around midnight, her aunts' large house had
burst into flames. Carl had been wakened, since his family lived
so near. Half the town had been there, and the whole of the fire
department. The house had burned for hours. In fact, it was still
on fire. And as far as anyone knew, there were no survivors.
That meant her three aunts, a cook, two parlourmaids and
Agnes, who – the police were assuming – had been the one who
had started the blaze.

'Oh,' Carla said in the dark. 'Oh. I can't take it in.'

'Go back to sleep. I only called up because I didn't want you
to hear through somebody else. My uncles are going to be
handling most of the paperwork, I guess.'

'Shouldn't I go out there?'

'No. There's nothing you could do. There's just a big crowd of
people watching the place burn to the ground. It's OK about the
passport, by the way. Or maybe you won't want to go, now that
they've passed on.'

'I don't know,' she said. 'I'll have to think about it.' She said
goodbye and lay back in the bed. She wondered about Agnes
and whether the act of arson had been revenge for being cut out
of a new will. She thought about the three old women surrounded by fire, then she pushed that thought away and went
to sleep again.

* * *

In the first week they covered north and middle Germany and were headed towards the south. Uncle Theodore was always at some new address; he'd also sold a lot of his former property. Gisela evidently hadn't kept up with his movements as well as she'd imagined. All the telephone numbers Carl had unearthed were out of date. Even the exchanges were different. Sometimes the new occupants they met would become interested and dispense friendly information and advice, none of which was of any help in tracking down the missing relatives; or, at least, not during those first few days. But Carl usually managed to get another address out of the people they interviewed – his German was better than hers – and so they moved south.

'It's like the treasure-hunts my grandfather used to invent for us,' Carla said. 'At Easter, when we were children: you began with a poem that was a riddle. It led you to a certain place, where you'd find the next clue. And at the end there was a present.'

'Lots of candy? A chocolate egg?'

'No, we had that anyway. The present was usually a book.'

'Bavaria next,' Carl said. 'We've even got castles on the agenda.'

'Aunt Gisela told me the really big estates were in the east. Some of them were in Poland and Czechoslovakia.'

'So they're all collective farms by now?'

'One of them's a sanatorium and another one's a kind of health farm, where people can do their exercises in beautiful surroundings. It had a famous park.'

'Doesn't it make you feel strange to know that your family owns those places – that they're actually part of your inheritance?'

'No,' Carla said, 'definitely not. One ordinary apartment is going to be plenty for me. What makes me feel funny is knowing I've got all these relatives like Uncle Theodore and Aunt Regina, and I've never met them. And now I can't even find them.'

'We'll get you there,' he assured her. 'Plenty of time. I've got six weeks.'

'Five, now.'

'And we've got two good clues: Munich and Naples. Maybe we should split up for a couple of days. That might cut down on the time. How's your Italian?'

'It isn't. Only phrases from operas: *Ah, patria mia. Perfido amore.* And so on. That's about it.'

'And I can ask what time the train goes and how much things cost. What do you think? I could go there and phone you in Munich. OK?'

She thought it over while they ate lunch outdoors on a terrace crammed with iron tables, each of which had a striped parasol sprouting from a central bar that went up through the middle of the tabletop like the trunk of a tree. They were surrounded by Scandinavian and American tourists. Carla figured that she could find her way around another German city all right, but she wouldn't have any idea how to go about making a phone call from one country to another, between two languages, neither one of which was her own.

'All right,' she agreed.

'I'll miss you,' he said.

She smiled. He meant that he'd miss sleeping with her. All the time they were still in America, nothing had happened. And on the first night they'd spent in Germany, he'd come into her hotel room and that was that.

They'd visited one or two places not on the list: she'd always wanted to see Heidelberg, so they'd gone there and had their picture taken together with what seemed like hundreds of other tourists; there were Americans all over the town, even though the summer was almost over.

And they'd made a detour to a little church they'd been told about, which was supposed to be architecturally interesting. As they'd approached the place in their rented Volkswagen, Carla had suddenly seen the building; it stood on the top of a hill, among other gently rounded slopes planted with wheat that had already been harvested. The stooks were lined up in the fields, the sky embellished with puffy clouds, and the whole day was like an illustration from a volume of nursery rhymes. The church itself was of a dark, honey-coloured stone; the front looked like a Carlsbad clock one of her father's aunts had owned.

Most of the other tourists there had been German. They were taking photographs of the outside, and talking in lowered voices inside. As she and Carl entered, the change from bright light to the murky interior was abrupt. Carla had stood still. With one hand she'd held on to Carl. With the other she'd twiddled nervously at the small ruby ring her grandmother had given her in the spring.

'This way,' Carl had whispered. She'd followed him until they stood side by side, looking into a glass box let into the church wall. Inside the box was what Carla at first took to be a ceremonial robe laid out in splendour. And then all at once she realized that within the robe was a corpse. There had been fourteen of the things, each in its private showcase, all around the inner walls. They were supposed to be saints.

'I'll miss you, too,' she told him.

She got so lost in Munich, and so often lost, that she ended up taking taxis everywhere. It was pointless in any case; the two houses she was looking for, and of which she had several fine photographs, didn't exist. In one instance, the street itself was no longer apparent. Everything had been bombed and built over.

She walked around the museums and in the evening went out to a performance of a ballet. When she got back to her hotel, there was a message that Carl had telephoned. He called again at midnight.

'Any news?' she asked.

'Lots. And I've talked to Uncle Theodore.'

'Well, finally.'

'Not completely. I talked to him on the phone. He's in South America.'

'I don't believe it.'

'And he wants us to come see him.'

'Just hop across—'

'And he's arranging the flight and paying for everything. And,' he added, 'he says he's just dying to see you.'

They walked out of the airport into a thrashing crowd as noisy as a political demonstration. A lot of the people looked as if they were in fancy-dress. Everything suddenly seemed utterly strange to Carla – almost as though she'd been put into a different century. She didn't even have the sense that she might have known the place from pictures in newspapers or on television.

Carl held her by the arm. He had a way of nipping her upper arm with his hand so that his thumb made a large, painful bruise. She didn't complain. She thought that if he let go, they might become separated. And if that happened, she wouldn't stand a chance. The noise and crowd and heat would overwhelm her. She felt nearly ready to pass out as it was.

He found a porter and then a cab. They drove away from the airport, through part of the city and to a highway. She sat silent, his arm around her shoulders. The taxi turned off the main road and started to climb. They were going up into the mountains.

'Look,' he said.

She made an attempt to take in the landscape and the views, but she was too tired to appreciate anything. She tried to sleep. She wished they hadn't left Europe.

It was evening when she woke. The taxi had stopped and their luggage was being moved to a horse-drawn carriage. Carl shook her as she began to close her eyes again. When she saw the horses waiting and got a second look at the carriage, she said, 'My God, it's like one of those fairytale things.'

They both wanted to sit outside, up with the coachman, who kept signalling back towards the doors with his whip and repeating some instructions.

'What's he saying?'

Carl told her, 'He wants us to get in.'

'Why?'

The man put the whip down and made flapping movements with his hands.

'Owl?' Carl asked.

'Bats,' she said. 'I'll bet that's what it is. Let's go.' She climbed into the coach and sat down on the seat. As soon as Carl joined her, the wheels rolled forward. She said, 'This is unbelievable.'

'I guess the roads aren't very good.'

'If they're no good for a car, they'd be a lot worse for one of these things.'

'Pretty comfortable, actually. If Clark Gable could do it in a phone booth—'

'We could fall out on the doorstep before we realized we'd arrived. I could have bruises in a lot of new places.'

The night came down around them, the road grew bumpy. At one stage, while they were negotiating a sharp turn, something slapped hard against one of the windows from the outside. Carla was suddenly wide awake.

'A bat,' Carl said in a sinister voice. 'Coming to get you.'

'Couldn't have been. It was huge. Maybe it was a condor. Or a big rock.'

'A rock would break the window.'

'It's so dark,' she said. 'There isn't a light anywhere.'

They drove for half an hour more before they saw lights, which seemed from the outline to be coming from a castle of some kind.

'They don't have castles here,' he told her.

'Well, a big house. An enormous house. See?'

Carl put his face to the window. He didn't speak.

She said, 'I've got a feeling it's like something I've seen before. It looks a little like one of those photographs. Maybe they built it that way on purpose, as a copy of what they'd left behind. Carl?'

'It's big, all right,' he said.

'You slept well?' her great-uncle Theodore asked. In daylight he didn't look so peculiar. When she'd arrived – cold, sleepy, stumbling into the light – he'd struck her as odd, and incredibly old, and irretrievably foreign. She and Carl had been introduced to the entire indoor household, who were lined up in the front hall to meet them. The other great-uncle, Erwin, had appeared senile and dwarfish rather than – as now – diminutive and charming. And her great-aunt Regina, in a floor-length green and black dressing gown, had given an impression of dramatic malevolence; she now seemed merely grumpy and theatrical: a heavy-faced old woman who dyed her hair black, as she must have been doing for nearly forty years. She also wore, even at breakfast, a great deal of strong-coloured make-up. Another woman – a frail figure in white, who had gestured tentatively from a landing the night before – still hadn't come downstairs.

'I slept like the dead,' Carla said. 'Isn't Carl up yet?'

'Roderigo is showing him the estate. He woke early, with the others.'

She sipped her coffee. The first thing they'd done as she'd sat down was to warn her about the strength of their coffee.

She wondered why Carl hadn't come to her room. She didn't even know where he was sleeping. As soon as the servant had shown her to the room she was to have, he'd hurried Carl down the corridor, and that was the last she'd seen of him. She thought it was strange. He was only a recently acquired boyfriend, but the others didn't know that; they had been told that she and Carl were engaged. That was supposed to make the whole question of bedrooms easier and perhaps less offensive, if anyone thought that way about it.

'Was Roderigo the man with the moustache?'

'The manager, yes. They'll be back for lunch. And in the meantime, perhaps Kristel – '

'Kristel is in her study,' Regina said.

'Or Regina?'

'I have to do my exercises.'

'And I, unfortunately, am occupied with business matters, but – '

'I should be delighted', Erwin said, 'to show little Carla the house and gardens.'

Erwin was waiting for her in the hall when she came down from brushing her teeth. She was beginning to get a better idea of the structure of the house. It was built in storeys, on several levels of the mountainside. The gardens too climbed up and down screes of rock into which stone steps had been cut. There was a wooden handrail that would have been useless if anybody had really needed to lean on it. Uncle Erwin skipped along nimbly at her side. For a man of his age he appeared astonishingly agile and supple in his movements. All the great-uncles and aunts of the family must have been hitting eighty at least, possibly ninety and upwards.

'Did the family build the house?' Carla asked.

'No, it was here before. It was a convent, or a monastery, or something like that. And a fortress. So often these places are like that: they have some treasure, and so they have to be in a position to defend it. There are a great many sacred buildings in the area from the same period. Most of them are partly ruined. They were lucky to have water here. That's why they survived so long. We added a lot, of course. Look.' He raised his arm towards the windows and towers above them. He started to explain which walls had been added when. Carla lost interest.

He went on, 'There are three main gardens. Everything else is extra. The vegetables are over on the other side. Now, be careful and watch where you put your feet. The mist comes up and makes the rock slippery. And there's a kind of moss – that can be just like ice when it's raining.'

He led her down a stone staircase between two walls dappled green and grey with lichen, and into an arcade of white-blossomed bushes. Everything in the first garden was white.

The second garden was almost all full of red flowers, though there were pink and orange shades too, and some yellow. The last garden was purple, blue and grey. 'We wanted black,' Erwin said, 'but so few flowers are truly black and the only ones we could think of won't grow here.'

'A black garden? Why?'

'Because of the flag, of course. Red, white and black.'

'I thought the flag here was – '

'The German flag, Carla dear.'

'Oh? Well, I guess now you've got the American flag instead. And England and France.'

'Yes. Unfortunate, but it will have to do.'

He walked her down to the front of the house, where they climbed into a carriage. The sides of the vehicle were open but there was a canvas top. Erwin gave orders to the driver in a language Carla didn't understand. As they started to move, she told him about the night before and about the bird, or whatever it was, that had bumped into them.

'Probably an owl,' Erwin said.

'We thought it might have been a bat.'

'Bats never make a mistake like that. They have their own system of radar. But an owl, or another kind of bird, might have been caught by the shine of the windows.'

'Do you get a lot of bats around here?'

'Thousands. And they're the real thing, you know – the vampire bats. They come into the fields at night and attack the cattle. And also the horses. We have to be careful. Of course the local people here say that we're vampires, too – our family.'

'Why on earth?'

'It's a figure of speech. Because we're rich. We suck the blood from the poor. At least, according to them. The truth is that we're civilized and educated and they're just ignorant peasants. And we pay them to do work for us.'

'You own the land they live on?'

'That's right. And so do you. You're a member of the family.'

She was shown a model village, a rug-weaving factory and a fish farm. The workers were Indians of all ages. A lot of them were very light-skinned. Most of the adults, both men and women, had a scar on their foreheads. Carla didn't hear a single laugh, or even any talking, among them. They worked slowly, with concentration.

Erwin made a detour so that she could see what was happening in a pool at the other end of the hatcheries. He led her up close. A large, jittery crowd pressed forward behind her. When two men emptied a pail of scraps into the water, the pool appeared to boil with activity. The crowd moaned, at once sickened and gratified. 'It's the fish,' Erwin said. 'They're like piranhas.'

'You breed them?'

'Not really. We like to keep the pool full. Everybody knows what can happen to whatever falls in. The idea of being deliberately pushed in, or even thrown, is one that fascinates our employees. They seem to regard it as a form of insurance we hold over them – a warranty of their good behaviour. I understand that mothers even threaten their babies with it.'

'But, that's terrible.'

'No, no. It's like a legend now. It's, ah, a focus of attention to which other things are referred. You understand?'

'I don't think so,' Carla said.

'Well, it doesn't matter. Let's just say – everyone would miss the pool if we decided to get rid of it. And the people who'd miss it most of all are the ones who are the most afraid of getting thrown into it.'

They spent the rest of the morning looking at meadows and pastures and views that spread away from them like an ocean of cultivated land. The family holdings appeared to be of about the same acreage as the state of Connecticut, or possibly even more extensive than that.

'And the forests,' Erwin added. 'We sometimes speak of them as the jungle. And all the places where you can find butterflies. Kristel is our great lover of butterflies. She can show you.'

'Was that the woman in the shawl?'

'That was the housekeeper, Maria. Kristel didn't come downstairs last night. She hasn't been well.'

'Oh? I hope it's not serious.'

'It's never serious,' he said. 'She likes the pose. Her mother was an invalid – romantic and glamorous: had hundreds of lovers. One always assumed that her fatigues were brought on by an excess of amours. Or perhaps a heightened artistic sensibility. I remember her very well – a marvellous woman. Poor Kristel isn't quite up to that standard. And she doesn't have the acting talent.'

'Oh,' Carla said again. Erwin gave directions to the driver to turn the horses and they went through a gully that was bursting forth in yellow bushes even high up, where it didn't look as if the roots would have anything to hold on to.

They reached the house again and were let off near another walled garden, so that Carla could be shown the vegetables. She stepped over a low-growing branch of pink flowers and clutched at the corner of a stone outcrop. They had followed the paths around to the other side, where the vegetables joined up with the flower gardens. The blue air beyond rose above them like another mountain. The combination of flowers and talk and the steep climb between dangerous turnings was beginning to confuse her. She said, 'You know, I think I've still got a little jet-lag left over. I feel sort of dizzy.'

Erwin put out a hand to steady her. 'How selfish of me,' he said. 'I should have thought. It's probably the altitude, too – most people feel that straight away.'

She didn't see Carl until just before lunch. He was coming down the main staircase as she was going up. She asked, 'What happened last night?'

'There you are,' he said. 'This place is driving me crazy. I couldn't find my way back to your room, and then I almost got lost again when somebody turned out the lights. Jesus, did you hear the crying?'

'No.'

'Roderigo says everybody thinks it's a ghost.'

He started to tell her about the tour he'd been given. She thought how healthy he looked, and how happy. He even seemed a little too cheerful – like a commercial for a cereal. He told her, 'This place is fantastic. The whole thing. It's like a private empire. Really.'

'And by rights Aunt Gisela should have had her share of it. Maybe it was all hers.'

'First I've heard.'

'She told me that. She said: "Theodore stole the Treasure from me."'

'She was kind of gaga towards the end of her life.'

'"Count Walter's Treasure" – that's what she called it. At first I thought it was her way of alluding to something else, like her emotions or her honour. You know. But she would have been almost a generation older – well, not quite that much, but I think she was too old to have had any kind of an affair with him when she was young. She was way up in her nineties – at least ten years older, so it couldn't have been in her youth: he'd have been too young for her back then.'

He said, 'I know these older women that keep on moaning about being ruined by younger men.'

'Is that right?'

'Wishes.'

'Carl, has Uncle Theodore said anything to you about how long we're invited for?'

'It's indefinite.'

'My work isn't indefinite,' she said.

Over luncheon Uncle Theodore talked about the history of the estate and the founding of the family fortunes in that part of the world. Regina listened to him without comment. She shovelled her food purposefully into her mouth and chewed. Aunt Kristel had risen from her sickbed in order to attend the meal. She had shied away from both young people, saying, 'Please – if you'll forgive me: my hands hurt today.' And she had placed the hurting hands in her lap. 'Some days', she murmured, 'are worse than others.' Carla was just as glad to avoid the physical contact. Kristel's whitely desiccated face and hands were alarming: they had a leprous look.

She shot a glance at Carl but he was turned to Theodore in an attitude of interest and expectation. She looked down at her plate. The meeting with her aunts and uncles was one she'd felt she had to have, but it was hard for her to believe that she was related to these people. They seemed grotesque. She couldn't understand how Carl was able to play up to them, unless he was simply impressed by their wealth. *To the end of the week*, she thought: and then she'd be saying goodbye.

'Goodbye?' Uncle Erwin said. 'But – we shouldn't dream of letting you go so soon.'

'I have to get back to my work.'

'Yes, the child is right,' Theodore agreed. 'We're retired. And the young have their own lives.' He sighed. 'But stay to the end of the week at any rate. We'll have a few parties. Show you around the neighbourhood and boast a little.'

'Yes, parties,' Kristel squealed. The onrush of gaiety made her look momentarily imbecilic as well as ill. She raised her afflicted hands in the air and made a few dancing movements with them.

'I'll send someone down to the village,' Theodore said. 'Have you any preference for a day? I'm afraid the best we can do is Tuesday or Thursday. Let's make it this Thursday. Then we'll be able to keep you a bit longer.'

'All right,' she said. Everyone around the table smiled. She wondered why she'd ever had the feeling that they might not be willing to let her go.

That afternoon she and Carl had tea with Theodore, who talked about the duties of running such a large estate and the difficulties of growing old without heirs. 'You have to leave everything to foundations,' he said, 'and do it in such a way that the next generation won't be forever quarrelling about what you really meant.'

Carla said that she agreed with her grandmother: you should just give your possessions away and let the other people do what they liked with them. She twisted and turned her grandmother's ring as she said so. It wasn't easy to speak up against Theodore.

'One or two trinkets', he told her, 'are hardly to be compared with a huge amount of land.'

'But the principle's the same. The future may be completely different. The way people live, the circumstances of their – '

'The future,' Theodore stated, 'can be controlled from the past. Good planning ensures that the future will be as one wants it. We have to look ahead, that's all.'

'No one's ever been able to do that.'

'I agree with your uncle,' Carl said.

'Oh?'

'Certainly. It's only a question of organization. It's political.'

'Really,' she said.

'That's right. And', he looked at Theodore as if for confirmation, 'the systematization of heredity.'

'What does that mean?'

'It means: the great thing about graduating from the Neanderthal and Cro-Magnon stages is that once you've got a good brain, you can get the people with less brains to work for you. And if you're only reproducing with your own kind, your people become more and more intelligent, while theirs become progressively stupid and degenerate, and finally unable to run their lives without being governed by someone else.'

'But does inheritance operate like that? I thought it was supposed to skip around; you know – the similarities show up on the tangent and between generations that are three or four steps apart.'

'No,' Carl said flatly. 'All you have to do is look at greyhounds and horses. It's a matter of breeding.'

Uncle Theodore nodded. He looked approvingly at Carl. It was easy to see where the theory had originated. Carla said, 'Even if that were true – which I don't believe – would it be right to deny people equality just because they're stupid or underbred?'

Theodore took over. 'It's definitely right', he answered, 'to prevent them from taking up a position of power for which they're completely unqualified.'

'If you change people's circumstances and upbringing and education, you change their qualifications.'

'No. There's nothing you can do with poor stock.'

She was irritated enough to push the argument further, even though it would break up the tea-drinking. She opened her mouth to begin and then saw that the others all sided with Theodore. It was better to drop the subject. She said, 'Well, I don't agree.'

Kristel giggled and said she'd always felt that debates on these big political subjects were best left to the men. Regina threw her a look of contempt.

'The future is our job,' Theodore said. 'As well as the present.'

Carla raised her cup to her lips. Maybe the mania for control – like the whole line of reasoning – was connected with the fact that these people had no generations to come after them. The future meant children. Now, at last, she was glad she didn't have any. She remembered one of the quarrels she'd had with her husband; suddenly she could even recall, as if echoed intact, the tones of their voices as they'd yelled at each other. 'When are you going to get pregnant?' he'd shouted. And she'd screamed back, 'When you stop sleeping around.' 'I'm not going to stop,' he'd told her. 'I like it. It's a hell of a lot more fun than you are right now.' And so forth. It had gone on and on. And all that time she'd wanted children, yet she'd known that no matter what he said, he'd walk out on her as soon as she had any. She hated him more than anything in the world and wished that she could kill him again and again – once wouldn't be enough.

She was gripping her teacup tightly and staring down at the rug. She still loved him, which made it worse. The marriage couldn't have ended any other way, but she kept catching herself at wishing: if only things had been different. The future might be determined by the past, but the present seemed to her always uncontrollable and chaotic.

Kristel finished her last cup of tea as she pressed flowers into the pages of a book for Erwin's collection. Regina occupied herself with some kind of crocheted scarf. And while Theodore took Carl upstairs to look at some old papers that concerned the estate, Carla walked up the opposite staircase, to her room. On her way she passed the three paintings that gave her the creeps: a landscape of blasted trees and ruined temples lit by a livid glare that made the stone columns look like old, naked legs; a still-life vase full of rotting flowers, with a cup and saucer sitting on the table in front of it; and a mythological scene that showed a convocation of centaurs: these bearded, hairy creatures were grouped in a circle, though most of them had their muscled backs towards the viewer, and within the tight huddle they formed, appeared to be doing some-thing singular, perhaps unpleasant, possibly unspeakably gross.

Regina had told her the names of the painters, who were apparently well-known. Regina was extremely proud of all three. They were, she said, prime examples of German culture.

Carl came to her room before they went down to dinner. He said, 'I won't see you tonight. Your uncle is initiating me into some kind of ceremony. It's for men only.'

'What kind of ceremony?'

'I don't know. Some club the ranchers have, maybe.'

'I hope it isn't anything political. From the way they've been talking, you might end up covered in swastikas.'

'Don't be silly.' He sounded as pompous and didactic as Theodore, but unlike Theodore, he wasn't the kind of man you could be afraid of. There was a hint of shiftiness about him. He'd probably done something crooked with her great-aunts' money, she thought. He'd probably been friendly with Agnes.

'What are you looking like that for?' he asked.

'I was remembering what you told me about older women,' she said. 'How they fell in love with younger men.'

'It isn't just the older ones here. It's all of them. Haven't you noticed? There are a lot of blond children on the estate. And grown-ups, too. Theodore told me: it's in our interest to have as many workers as possible. And it isn't as if they mind.'

'Who mind?'

'The women. They come to us naturally, of their own free will. They reject their own men.'

Us? she thought. She said, 'Why do they do that?'

'Because', he said, perfectly seriously, 'we're superior.'

It wasn't worth getting angry about, but the effort of putting up with him was beginning to wear her down. He was still good-looking and she still felt tolerance and a certain affection for his body, but not so much now for his face or voice. And all at once she wondered about the fire at her aunts' house: how it had really started, and if someone had deliberately set it, or had even been told to.

'I guess it's like the lobotomies,' he said. 'They think of it as medicine.'

'What's medicine? Are you talking about sex? What does lobotomy have to do with it?'

'When you took the tour with Erwin, didn't you see how many of the Indians have a scar right here on their foreheads?'

'Yes. It's the way they get rid of the poison from some kind of insect. It's trepanning, not lobotomy.'

'Whatever you want to call it. They go to Erwin, crowds of them, and ask him to do it. Theodore, too; Erwin taught him how. No insect bites, no infection – they just want the operation. And afterwards they feel better. A lot of them want it done over and over.'

'There isn't any reason for it? They aren't sick?'

'They're all completely well. I told you: they just want the operation. Apparently it goes way back. The Incas used to do it, too.'

'The Incas used to cut the hearts out and eat them.'

'That was the Aztecs.'

'I can't believe it.'

'It's all in the history books.'

'Jesus,' she said.

'I don't know. They really do feel better afterwards. And a lot of civilized people believe the same: they want somebody to run their lives, fix them up, change their luck.'

'That's horrible.'

'If it makes them happy?'

'It can't,' she said. 'To have an unnecessary operation can't make them happy.'

'But it does,' he told her.

Carla sat between Regina and Kristel on the back seat of a horse-drawn carriage. They were shielded by screen curtains and covered with a green canvas top, in spite of which she'd already been stung by a gnat.

They had a driver named Eusabio. He'd stopped the horses so that the ladies could admire the view. In the distance, outcrops of rock massed together into a chain of spiky hilltops. At the top of one of the high peaks was another monastery; they'd seen three already.

'Now, this is really interesting,' Regina said.

Kristel murmured, 'I don't feel well.'

'I've got a bit of a headache myself,' Carla admitted.

'Nonsense,' Regina said. 'You'll both feel better once we've had some exercise.'

'I'm not walking all the way up there,' Kristel wailed. 'That's how Frieda got sick. You kept pushing her.'

Erwin turned around from the front seat and smiled at Carla. 'You mustn't think we're like this all the time,' he said.

'Oh, shut up,' Regina told him.

'Usually', he added, 'we're much worse.'

Regina rose from her seat. She climbed down to the ground. Erwin followed, saying that they'd be back soon. Eusabio drove the carriage forward slowly and stopped under the shade of some trees. They waited. Carla fanned herself with a piece of paper she'd found in her purse; she always kept a supply of paper by her in case she wanted to jot down an idea for a design.

'I hate these places,' Kristel said. 'They aren't my idea of Christianity at all. I remember the way churches used to be – the way they still are, on the other side of the world. God knows what the people here really believe. They're all like animals.'

'I got the impression they were very devout.'

'They like ceremonies. They love all these ceremonies about death and entombment. The ideas, the ideals, mean nothing to them.'

The glare coming off the rocks was beginning to make Carla sleepy and slightly dizzy. She looked down at the fan she was holding, and noticed that on part of the paper she'd begun a picture of one of her cat-boxes; the paper must have been in her bag for months: the drawing divided the sitting cat at a point lower than the one she'd finally chosen. And the completed boxes had been put into production before the previous Christmas. She considered telling Kristel about the German church of the fourteen saints. But it wasn't worth trying to shock these people.

'I feel sick,' Kristel said.

'Was Frieda the one who couldn't walk? Was she always – '

'Healthy as a horse till her eighty-sixth birthday, when she made a pig of herself on Elvas plums and brandy.'

'Didn't she have a disease like – '

'Oh, everybody knows what was wrong with her. Disappointed in love, that's all. And Regina – well. She was the scandal.'

And you? Carla thought.

'Regina would still be a scandal if anybody'd take her. It's a disgrace. And now she's so righteous.'

'And you?'

'Me?'

'Do you like living here?'

'Oh. Of course. I'd rather be back home, naturally, but this was where Theo wanted to take us.'

'Where's home?'

'Berlin, Dresden, Leipzig.'

'And the last time you were there?'

'I went back once on a visit with Erwin in 1931. We had a lovely time.'

'I see,' Carla said.

'I love parties. Are you looking forward to yours?'

'My what?'

'Your initiation ceremony.'

'Oh? Initiation into what?'

'Into the family.'

'Is that the same kind of thing Carl was doing last night?'

Kristel looked suddenly as if she'd said more than she should have, and knew that it was too late to do anything about it. She flapped her hands, laughed, and said she had an idea that the business with Carl was some sort of contest that had to do with the Indians.

'Like what?' Carla asked.

Kristel shrugged. She didn't know, she said. And maybe, Carla thought, she didn't.

'But I've seen your dress, and it's beautiful. It's just wonderful. It's silk and satin and all covered with little glittering jewels and shining white, like a wedding dress.'

'Oh?'

'Yes. Right down to the floor. And there's a veil that goes with it.'

Carla turned her head. Kristel was looking straight out into the landscape; her face glowed with eagerness. It was impossible to tell if she was lying, or remembering some other event, or imagining a thing that had never been.

'And you'll be wearing the family jewels. Including the Treasure – they had such a time getting it away from Gisela before we left home.'

She caught Carl as he was turning out of the hallway leading from her landing. 'What's going on?' she said.

He was in evening clothes. Something about them didn't look right. They fitted perfectly, but seemed antiquated, especially the jacket. 'Aren't you ready yet?' he said. 'I thought you were trying on your dress. We aren't supposed to see each other.'

'Carl, what is all this?'

'It's just to make them happy. Some kind of pageant-thing they do. The Indians believe it makes the grass grow, or something.'

'You're kidding.'

'Anyway, hurry up, will you? We don't have much time. And I want a drink first.' He ran on down the stairs, moving easily, his head up, not having to look down at his feet, which she always had to do on staircases.

She went to her room and began to pack. She started with the dresser drawers and the medicine chest in the bathroom. After that, it was only her two dresses and the trousers and extra skirt.

She opened the wardrobe door and stepped back. A mound of shiny white material bounced out at her – part of the lower half of a very long dress. It was like uncovering a light. And there seemed so much more of it than should belong to a single dress. She tried to push it in again, so that she could get to her clothes. The voluminous heaps of it sprang back at her. The whole garment reminded her of a filled parachute and a news-reel she'd once seen, that had shown a landed airman who'd had to fight with his still-billowing chute. It was all over her. But as she reached up to squash some of the material into place, she caught sight of the bodice, still on the hanger, and stopped. She'd never seen anything like it: delicate lace, interwoven with tiny pale jewels in leaf and flower patterns, criss-crossed by knotted and curled ribbons in all shades of creamy white: tinted in pastel colours like the dawn.

As she stood there examining the workmanship of the dress, there was a knock at the door and Regina stepped into the room. 'I'll help you with it,' she announced. 'You'll need some-one to snap up the inside straps, otherwise the folds won't lie right. The others are no use – they always get so hysterical about parties.'

'This must have taken years to make,' Carla murmured. 'Hundreds of people must have worked on it.'

'Only about ten, I think.'

'Where does it come from?'

'From here. It's been in the family for generations.'

'When was it – '

'Hurry up,' Regina ordered. 'Take off your clothes.'

The door opened again. Kristel and the housekeeper, Maria, burst in. Kristel looked even more sickly than usual – her skin was almost like a cheese going bad; but Maria was grinning with excitement. She made a grab at the buttons of Carla's blouse. Carla pulled away.

'Calm down, Maria,' Regina said. 'Here, hold the train free.'

Carla began to undress. She kept her underclothes on, and her sandals. Regina and Maria stood on chairs and lifted the dress down over her head.

'The shoes,' Kristel pointed out.

'Nobody's going to see the shoes,' Regina said. 'The dress is too long on her, anyway.'

'And the Treasure. My God, how could we have forgotten it?'

'I didn't forget,' Regina said. 'Hold her hair up, will you?'

They dragged her hair up and back, and began to stick hairpins into it. They jammed the veil comb on top and batted the netting out of the way; it floated backward like a ghostly shadow of herself. Kristel turned around and took a bottle and glass from a bag she'd left near the door. She poured out a liquid that looked like sherry, and handed the glass to Carla. 'Drink this,' she said. 'It's traditional.'

Carla was reluctant, but the drink smelled good.

'Go ahead,' Regina told her. 'Be careful not to spill.'

Carla drank.

She drank three glasses while the other women fussed over her – shoving rings on to her fingers, skewering diamonds into her sleeves, pinning and clipping sapphires across the headband of her veil. When they were ready at last, she felt drunk. They guided her out of the room, holding her skirts to protect them as she squeezed sideways through the doorway. They led her along a corridor, down a staircase and to a landing bordered by a balustrade. Down below she could see a congregation of people and heard the hum of their voices. Far off in the background she picked out Carl, who was talking to her great-uncle Theodore. She felt like yawning. Over in the right-hand corner a group of men with musical instruments sat in chairs. Such a large gathering, she thought: what was it about? And what was she doing there at all, surrounded by these weird old women? She should be at home, designing toys. Any minute now she'd begin laughing the silly laugh that came over her when she hit the best stage of inebriation – the first, where she felt terrific.

'You wait here with her,' Regina said. 'I'll be right back.'

'Where are you going?' Carla asked.

'To get the Treasure.'

'Better hurry up, before I fall asleep.'

'You shouldn't have given her the third glass,' Regina said to Kristel. 'Idiot.' She stomped away, turning abruptly and entering a room just beyond the corner. The band started to tune up. Kristel snivelled miserably; she muttered that her hands were hurting.

Carl looked up. Although he was so far away, Carla could tell that he was staring at her with an especially expectant, approving look. Some of the other people below had also caught sight of her, or rather, of the dress. The band gave out a few screeching chords, pulled itself together and swung into a jaunty tune. Regina came swishing back around the edge of the bannisters. She was holding a box covered in black velvet. She handed it to Carla, saying, 'Here. Put it on.'

Carla lifted the lid. It snapped open so that the contents were hidden from the others, but she could tell that in any case their attention was all on her face. She stared downward. 'What is it?' she asked.

'The largest pearl ever discovered,' Regina said importantly. 'Absolutely perfect, unique, and – of course – priceless.'

Carla smiled drunkenly down into the box, at the black velvet stand, the heavy, glittering linked chain, the elaborate gold and enamel setting, and inside it the large sunken blob of shrivelled brown matter that resembled a piece of burned meat.

'Well?' Regina said.

'Wonderful,' she answered. 'Priceless.'

People to People

Herb, Dave, Sherman and Joe sat around the table in Herb's hotel room. He was the only one who lived out of town. At first, after college, they'd all left. Then the three had returned. Herb had worked in Ohio for a while, and in Wisconsin, before settling in Illinois.

They had had wives and families, divorces, remarriages. Sherman was the only one whose marriage – so far – remained stable.

'I wish it was just to say hi,' Herb said. 'Have a couple of drinks, see a show, play a game of poker, talk about old times. I'm afraid I've got bad news. I've heard from Bill.'

'So?' Dave said. 'Last time I heard from Bill, he was campaigning to save the Indians or the jungles, or something like that. It's always bad news in his book.'

'I've got the letter here.' Herb pulled an envelope from his breast pocket, put on his reading glasses and took the letter out. *'Dear Herb,'* he announced, *'I've written this in my mind many times and I've wanted to, even more times. All those years I was in South America, the business about Carmen was preying on my mind.'*

'Oh, Jesus,' Joe said. 'That son of a bitch.'

'He spells it with an A,' Herb said: '"Praying on my mind."'

'Let's see that.' Dave held out his hand.

'Wait . . . on my mind. I never felt right about it, as you know.'

'That dumb bastard,' Joe said.

'It was like a cloud hanging over my life. I think it was the reason why I never got married.'

'Good excuse, anyway,' Dave said.

'But now I've found a wonderful girl. We were married last month. I hope you'll believe me when I say my life is completely changed. I thank God that I have lived long enough to experience this great happiness and at last to know the peace and wisdom of the Church of The Redeemer, which we both belong to.'

'Holy shit,' Joe said. 'One of those California cults.'

'Wait for the punchline, kids. You want me to go on? *I have talked everything over with Nancy (my wife) and she agrees with me that we wouldn't be worthy of God and His gifts to us if we continued to hide the truth.*'

'Oh God,' Sherman said. 'Not at this late date. He can't do it.'

'I am sure in my heart that this is the right thing to do. But I wanted to talk to you first, because I think we should all give ourselves up together. Please let me know as soon as possible what your thoughts about this are, since I am not going to feel right till we get it straight. OK. That's it.'

'That dumb fink,' Dave said. 'He gets religion and they slam us in the can for the rest of our lives. After twenty years.'

'He can't do it,' Sherman said. 'There's a statute of limitations.'

'For murder?' Joe asked.

'It wasn't murder. It was an accident.'

Herb said, 'Right. Now, listen. I figure old Bill hasn't stood up and told the multitude yet, only Nancy. So, I wrote straight back and said: yes, I understood because it was preying on me too, but I hadn't even worked out how to tell my wife and I thought it would be a good thing for all of us to talk about it in private before doing anything. I asked him to set a date and to bring Nancy – she'd be able to give us the woman's point of view. And he wrote back to say fine: they're coming about a month after Easter. Here, a hotel right down the street. I've got them a room and everything. And now I want to ask you all: what do we do when they get here?'

There was a long pause while Sherman put his hands over his eyes and Dave lit a cigarette. Joe jumped up from his seat; he stamped his feet and shook his shoulders angrily. He made punching motions with his fists.

Herb put the letter back inside its envelope and into his pocket. 'Well?' he asked.

'We kill them,' Joe said.

'Don't be funny,' Sherman told him.

'You got a better idea? What else can we do? They're religious nuts. There isn't any way you can deal with that. They're going to go to the cops and send us up the river to make everything jake with the Lord and save their consciences. We've got to.'

'This is why I thought we'd better get together,' Herb said.

'The first thing to establish is whether the guy's serious, and the second is – if he is, how we stop him. I'm telling you: I don't intend to have all that brought up again.'

'Me neither,' Dave said. 'Sherm?'

'No,' Sherman said. 'I don't think it's necessary to start talking about killing anyone, though.'

'You wait,' Joe said. 'You'll come to it. You all will.'

'I have a feeling,' Herb said, 'that a lot is going to depend on the girl. Nancy.'

Dave said, 'She sounds like a creep.'

'How do you get that?'

'Some religious female.'

'People can be religious for all sorts of reasons, and from a lot of different motives. This new-fangled church they belong to – the Church of The Redeemer: that should tell us something.'

'He's a dope,' Joe said flatly. 'He always was.'

'This isn't a traditional church. It's some kind of offshoot. On the perimeter.'

'Ecclesiastically off-Broadway,' Sherman said. 'Back to hellfire and cleanliness. Come back, Darwin, and say it again, louder. Christ Almighty, they're taking over the country. Now they want to teach it in the schools.'

'That's just an election gimmick,' Dave said.

'We get a President who knows his way around the Hollywood back lot and he didn't even bother to see that movie about the monkey trial.'

'What would you say he was like before?' Herb asked.

'Before getting to be President?'

'What was Bill like before this girl converted him? At least, I've been assuming she was the one.'

'A worrier,' Dave said. 'Nervous and worried, and couldn't ever pull himself together when he had to, or couldn't relax and enjoy himself. Had this thing about his parents and his child-hood. No good with girls, either. Always worried everything would go wrong. Unless he was drunk. Then he was fine.'

'Kind to animals,' Sherman said. 'Good with old people. Not so good with children. He froze up when people were rude to him. He ran on rails.'

'He was scared,' Joe said. 'He was scared shitless all the time. He was the one that panicked.'

'That was only once,' Herb said.

'But it showed what he was like.'

'Well, I sort of got the same impression about him: that he was somebody who was afraid of a lot of things. Stepping over his own feet half the time, afraid of living his life, of finding out what his possibilities were, letting rip. Which means, maybe he'd be easy to frighten.'

'No good,' Joe said. 'You ease up for a minute on that kind and all of a sudden they're more afraid of somebody else instead and they're talking all about whatever it was you wanted to keep quiet. It's got to be permanent.'

'What was he most scared of?'

'Carmen,' Sherman said. 'That's why it was so bad when it happened.'

'OK. We wait till they get here. Or do we map something out? Like I said, it looks to me like it's serious. I wouldn't have gotten you all together otherwise.'

'I could do it easy,' Joe said. 'I've still got my guns. But—'

'I don't like this kind of talk,' Sherman said.

'But I'd want all of you to be in on it some way. I mean, I'm not going to go in there alone and come out with the scalps and have the cops saying, "Where were you when the lights went out?"'

'You'd kill a woman?' Dave asked.

'If it's me or them, I'd kill anybody,' Joe said. 'Wouldn't you?'

'Bill is one thing. I wouldn't like it, but if he's really going to put us behind bars, so be it. But a girl – that doesn't seem right.'

'She could go to the cops just like him. She's the one pushing him to clear his conscience. She's got it coming to her.'

'I don't want to listen to this,' Sherman said. He stood up.

Herb said, 'Take it easy. We've got to decide something today. And we've all got to be together on it. We're all affected by this.'

'I don't think there's any need to talk about killing.'

'No, there may not be. But you can't afford to be so squeamish that we let the question drop till they're here in town talking about how good we'll feel when we go to the cops. Are you really prepared to let it happen?'

'I just think there's got to be some other way.'

'OK. Sit down and think of one.'

The five of them – Herb, Dave, Sherman, Joe and Bill – had had rooms in the same college dorm, on the same staircase. On the ground floor, down the hall from Herb, was a boy they hadn't noticed the year before, when they'd been in their Freshman dorms. His name was Jeff and he was good-looking, rich, spoiled and a snob. He arrived in a white sportscar which was his own, not his parents', and had all kinds of expensive and desirable objects delivered to his rooms – the best ones in the building – which he occupied alone, and which looked out on the tree-lined street. He had visitors. While his neighbours were still trying to find girls to go out with who'd say yes, Jeff was entertaining women who were working, possibly even married, and who – since his suite of rooms gave on to the street – could actually climb in and out of the living room at night.

He didn't bother to get to know anyone he thought wasn't going to be important. The five other boys near him he evidently considered not worth noticing.

One day Dave and Sherman were looking out of the window and saw Jeff walking across the path below.

'Do you suppose Jeff stands for Geoffrey?' Sherman asked.

'I wouldn't put it past him,' Dave said.

It was quite a while afterwards that someone looked him up in the Freshman yearbook and discovered his first two names to be 'C. Jefferson'. After that, there were bets on what the 'C' stood for. A friend of a friend, who had access to files in the Dean's office, did the rest.

They could hardly believe their luck. Joe actually didn't believe it for days. 'It's a girl's name,' he said.

'Well, his family's part Cuban or Spanish, or something,' Dave told him. 'It's probably one of those names that can be for both girls and boys.'

Within hours they were calling the name at Jeff from their windows. He didn't react. The next time he passed by, it was, 'Hey, Carmen Miranda.' He shouted back, 'Screw you.' Over the next few days he called out other things, phrases not in common use at the time – obscenity and gutter-language that the middle classes hadn't yet taken up as a fashion. The five boys yelled it back.

But of course all the time they were leaning out of their windows shouting 'Asshole' and 'Shitface' and asking why he didn't do such-and-such with so-and-so, they knew the thing that hurt the most was simply his own real name: Carmen, which he'd tried to disguise and hide at the beginning.

The crowd of them battled along that way from September through to the spring. Then, just before exam time, everyone was busy. They studied and they went out, saw movies, planned parties.

There was one large panty-raid on a neighbouring women's college. The raids were an imported custom from larger, rowdier universities that had already abandoned the practice and were more interested in reviving others, like goldfish-swallowing and crowding into telephone booths.

And the parties began. Some boys were drunk for days at a time. There was vomit on the staircases, loud music at night, mobs of talking, laughing, dancing people giving parties or looking for parties, or left behind. A friend of Herb's said he'd found the most beautiful girl one night, who couldn't remember where she was, and said she couldn't remember her name, either, and left before the morning without even giving him a phone number.

You were supposed to check people in and out in the usual way, but everyone knew that it was standard procedure to do both at the same time. Many girls were actually staying through the night, stealing out early the next day. There were a lot of girls in the building on the evening of Rockwell's party. Rockwell lived across the courtyard. The party was huge. There was hardly room to contain all the guests on his side of the building; most of them kept getting lost, anyway. Herb, Dave, Sherman, Joe and Bill weren't invited because they'd gone to the first one: Rockwell was giving three parties – one for friends, one for formal and family connections, and the last, and biggest, for acquaintances. All night long people were passing out in the corridors or asking how to get back to the party. They were screaming and crying, laughing and singing. Rockwell's phonograph played Chubby Checkers, Dixieland, big-band swing and barrelhouse.

The five boys tried to work but ended up breaking out the liquor and having their own party instead. Near midnight Sherman and Bill went out for food and brought back cheeseburgers, submarine sandwiches, french fries, doughnuts and cheesecake. After that, they had some more to drink. They considered starting up a poker game or going out somewhere, or crashing Rockwell's acquaintance-party, or sneaking into the gym and going for a swim. The swim won.

'But first we go wake up Carmen and Dolores,' Joe said. 'Give them a little surprise.'

Everybody was pretty drunk by then and it sounded like a good idea. Dolores was the name they'd given Carmen's latest girlfriend – a redhead who wore high heels and, until the warmer weather had begun, a fur coat. The idea was to catch the two in bed. Everyone wanted to get a good look at Dolores.

'And we'll invite them along,' Dave said. 'Big swimming party in the buff. Dolores is a good sport, she won't mind. She's probably a call girl, does it all the time.'

They charged up the hallway and pounded on the door. Herb turned the knob and pushed. The door opened. He switched on the light. They squeezed in through the corridor and living room, into the bedroom.

Carmen was standing in the middle of the floor. He'd obviously just gotten up out of bed, where he'd been sleeping alone. He was naked and angry.

'What the hell is this?' he asked.

Joe said, OK, where was she, and started calling names. Sherman and Herb were laughing. Bill sat down on a chair. Dave headed towards the bathroom, saying she was probably hiding in there.

'Get out of here,' Carmen told them. He added a lot about their characters and at the same time picked up and threw a cushion that caught Dave on the side of the head and knocked him into a chest of drawers. He didn't seem to be afraid at all, nor in any way embarrassed about having no clothes on. He looked around for something else to throw.

Joe tried to tackle him at the knees. Carmen pushed him aside so he fell against a chair.

All five felt that the fight began because Carmen kept throwing things at them. Their only aim was to stop him. And since there were five of them, they soon managed to knock him down and sit on him, even though he was sober and they were drunk.

Sherman then said he felt terrible and needed some air. He wanted to go up on the roof. So did Herb. The others said they couldn't leave Carmen there alone. They decided to take him with them.

They dragged him up all four double staircases to the top, out the emergency door and on to the roof.

It was a warm night full of stars. The breath of greenery came to them out of the darkness, from the treetops around the building. Carmen, who had seemed for a while to be only semi-conscious, came to. He started to fight again. He landed quite a lot of lucky punches and ducked out from under blows that then hit the others. For a while the five friends were stumbling around and fighting each other.

They caught him because he had no clothes. He had worked his way over to the edge of the roof near the front entrance. On one side below them was a large tree. Later it occurred to Herb that perhaps Carmen had hoped to be able to climb over the guttering, shinny down a few feet, grab hold of a branch and get into the tree, where he'd be safe from them until morning.

But they thought he was trying to manoeuvre them around so that he could start pushing them over. Dave and Joe began to mutter about what they could do to him to teach him a lesson. Herb and Sherman were still laughing, and Bill was in hysterics: it sounded as if he was crying.

The group struggled, fell, and lurched forward: grunting, laughing and swearing. And then, all at once, they lost him. 'Look out,' Sherman said, and it was already happening. They hadn't realized just how close to the edge they were, but they knew it the moment he slipped away. He gave a little cry that must have been just before he hit – the kind of sound a man might make if he'd bumped into the furniture in the dark – and then they heard the thump, and silence afterwards.

The entranceway to the building was paved stone and lit at night from the lights over the doorways. By leaning out carefully, they could see him below, lying face down.

He didn't move. They were all sure he was dead, but Herb said they had to call an ambulance right away, and Sherman said definitely: an ambulance and the police.

Bill went berserk: the police couldn't, wouldn't – to be mixed up with the police – his family, never. Joe and Dave didn't like the sound of it, either. 'We just go back to your room and forget about it,' Joe said. 'It was an accident. They'll think he was taking LSD, trying to fly.'

'We'd better get off this roof,' Dave said. 'He's lying in the light down there. Anybody finds him, they're going to come on up here.'

They went back to Herb's room, had some coffee and talked

about it. Joe socked Sherman in the jaw to stop him from telephoning. They had some more to drink and then had to prevent Herb from leaving the room. The ones who didn't want to get mixed up with the police began to find reasons why the others should stay clear, too. 'It would ruin your career,' Dave told Sherman. To Herb he said, 'You don't think he's still alive, do you? Falling on stone? We get the ambulance and the cops, and there's some dead greaseball kid out there all beat up and no clothes on – are you kidding?'

'Son of a bitch had it coming to him,' Joe said.

Bill stared down at the floor and said nothing. He drank three cups of coffee and fell asleep on Herb's fold-up sofa.

At about an hour before dawn, Joe and Dave went back to their rooms. Sherman and Herb slept. They slept all through the morning till noon, when there were loud knocks and poundings on all the doors in the hall.

The police didn't believe the drugs theory, although according to the rumours going around, they tested the body for all kinds of things. They also went into Carmen's rooms, where they found everything broken and about twenty girls and boys lying on the floor, in the bed, chairs, couches and wherever they could find space; they had moved in when someone saw the light on and the door open; their fingerprints were everywhere, their drinks all over the rug – they'd danced, made love, thrown up, smoked marijuana and left the shower on for six hours.

But despite the orgiastic behaviour of Rockwell's invited and uninvited acquaintances, what really shocked everyone speculating about Carmen's death was the fact that he had been naked. The bruises and scratches covering his body were incidental: they were evidence of violence, whereas the nakedness appeared to be a sign of erotic activity of some sort. And it was mainly as a result of the wild rumours which immediately sprang up that all five students were at first glad they had chosen to keep quiet. No one, they realized, would believe the truth. It looked too bad. It looked suspicious. It also, they came to see, looked deliberate.

They were never suspected, although they were questioned, but so was everyone else in the house. They said there had been too much coming and going to notice anything, that the racket had gone on just about all night, that they'd been drinking too and playing the phonograph, and that all they could say for certain was that when they went out for cheeseburgers and came back, there wasn't anybody lying on the ground in front of the entrance.

Carmen's uncle, a surprisingly young man called Earl-Somebody, came up to the college a few days later. He brought a dark-haired, intense-looking girl with him, who bore a slight facial resemblance to the dead boy; she was a cousin and her name was Lisa. Most of the time she sat in the uncle's car, or paced up and down. Whenever she had to wait for too long, she got up and walked around like an animal in a cage: on the sidewalk, in the corridors, in a room.

Earl himself came and asked them a lot of questions, among which were ones about friends, drugs, women, quarrels, money troubles. They told him they'd liked Jeff fine, only he'd kept himself apart from everyone else. The only close friends he'd seemed to want were the women they'd seen him with and they didn't know who any of those were, except to say that they hadn't looked like college girls – they'd worn a lot of make-up and had their hair all specially done; and the shoes . . . you know.

'Sure,' Earl said. 'I get you.' He thanked them all, and, as he left, asked a couple of questions about traffic directions. Herb walked to the entrance with him and then out on to the street, where the car was parked. He told him how to get across town.

Earl said, 'Somebody hated him a lot.'

'How do you figure that?'

'He was beat up real bad.'

'Maybe when he hit the ground—'

'No. The cops told me it was all done before that. And more than one guy, definitely.'

'Well, as far as I know, everybody in the building got along with him. The only thing I can think of is something to do with his girls.' Herb described how people could be let into those ground-floor rooms from the windows on the street. Then he said, 'But you can't imagine what it was like with that party going on. There were fights and jokes going on all night long. The noise was just unbearable. We turned up the volume as high as we could, and the walls were still shaking with it. And everybody was pretty drunk. So, it doesn't have to have been on purpose. It could have been some kind of a dare that got out of control.'

'Except', Earl told him, 'that he hadn't had anything to drink. That seems strange.'

'Yes, it does,' Herb agreed. 'The whole thing seems strange.'

Earl held out his hand. Herb shook it. For the first time he realized that he had destroyed part of his life: from that point onward all mention of the incident, or the time surrounding it, would call up the fabricated substitute: the safe, untrue version.

There was worse to come. After a week, Herb and Sherman began to feel that the two guilty ones – the ones who had really wanted all along to kill Carmen – were Joe and Dave. And Joe and Dave felt that though they were all in it equally, the others were looking at them in a funny way and not really backing them up.

Bill started to have nightmares, or rather, one particular bad dream that kept repeating. In it, he was walking along without any worries until suddenly he came to the edge of a cliff he hadn't noticed at all, and he began to slide towards it. He started to go faster and faster, until he fell over the edge, waking up in terror. He went to the other four for help, but they only told him to relax and forget about everything. Dave gave him some sleeping pills a girlfriend had let him have. They didn't work when they were supposed to, but knocked him out the next day, taking effect so quickly that Bill said he was scared about what they must be doing to his brain. He stopped taking them, lost weight, and developed a nervous twitch in his chin. He said that all he could think about was that they were going to get caught, and then they'd be in a lot more trouble than they would have been if they'd reported the accident straight away. It was, he said, like hit-and-run drivers.

The five of them had many urgent, whispered arguments. Bill sat with his hands squeezing and squirming together while the others told him that if only he could pull himself together enough to get through the next couple of weeks, he'd be able to go away for the summer as usual, and from then on everything would be easy.

Suddenly the final exams were on top of them. Even Bill put aside the memory of Carmen. They all got through somehow. And afterwards, Herb called a meeting. He said they'd have to face it: they'd have to be careful. For the rest of their lives they would never be able to go on a real bender, in case they spilled the truth. They'd never be able to let their guard down completely with anybody – not with a girl, not even if they got married. You could never tell when somebody else would repeat a thing, and no one had the right to put the others in danger like that. 'It's going to be hard,' he said. 'I hadn't realized how much I'd want to talk about it to someone who'd be sympathetic and make it all right. But I'm telling you – never. Not to a doctor or your mother, or anybody. Think it over and you'll see I'm right.'

They thought about the matter all summer long. They changed towards each other. It wasn't exactly that they began to think of the others with hatred, but the friendship was broken. Herb and Sherman still liked each other, as did Dave and Joe. But Bill ended up on the outside of both groups.

In the fall they all asked for different room-mates. And right after college, they all moved away from town. It took several years before any of them wanted to come back.

Of course they told other people about it. Twenty years is a long time and it's possible to describe an accident as if you had been on the sidelines, rather than saying: *I helped to kill somebody*.

They told their wives. And their versions of the incident made it seem like a practical joke gone wrong, a group disaster that had taken place while alcohol had temporarily removed everyone's responsibility. By the time they were married, the event had decreased in importance, anyway. It had ceased to frighten them because of possible consequences, but it had also lost its power to make them afraid of themselves.

Only Bill was different. He didn't marry. He lost touch for many years. He never – so he said to them later – told anyone. He lived with the memory until he couldn't stand it any longer, and then he broke. What finally did it was the years he spent in South America.

He was working as an adviser on government agricultural schemes. Men he had known well would be missing from their jobs one morning and he'd assume that they had been arrested either by the police or the army, or a semi-official government organization – guerrilla fighters or small city groups of terrorists who had been at the receiving end of the official murder and torture squads. During his last two years, foreigners were particularly at risk, Americans more than others.

Perhaps Bill himself was left alone because he was in-drawn, didn't speak much, didn't have many friends. He had no religious thoughts, either – at least, he wasn't aware of having any, nor at that time did he have a regular girlfriend. Women had stopped wanting to know him at about the time when he had lost the ability to take part in his own life. He said later that it was like being a sleepwalker.

He was woken up by his sense of danger. Fear was all around; it was shining out of the streets. He knew all at once that if he stayed, they'd get him no matter how innocuous he appeared. Political groups like the ones around him were entirely uninterested in who was innocent or guilty, and of what. They were only intent on producing more fear. The falling-dream he'd had years before gave way to one in which people pounded on the door and called his name: coming to get him, as he and his friends had gone to get Carmen and found him naked.

He wasn't so completely panic-stricken that he was ready to abandon all his belongings. He spent two hours making arrangements to leave, telephoning packing companies, the bank, his employers. He told everyone that his parents – who had died five years before – were in the hospital, were badly injured and needed him to be with them immediately and take care of them for a while.

At the airport he was shaking all over. The fear was worse than anything he'd known before. He was prepared now to go to an ordinary American jail and give up a few years of his life; but to be beaten, tortured and humiliated was something he realized he wasn't going to be able to live through. He still had something of himself to lose; if it went, he wouldn't be human any more.

He had the jitters all during the plane trip. When they put down in Texas, he stood by one of the airport watercoolers and drank one paper cup of water after another. He collected his suitcases and sat in the airport for two hours. He had no idea where he should go.

At last he grew hungry, had a meal in one of the airport cafeterias and decided to take a bus out of town.

He spent over twenty-four hours on different buses. In the end, he couldn't go any farther. He sat down at a bus stop in the middle of a small town he'd never seen before, and collapsed.

He wasn't very loud. The tears poured silently over his cheeks. He sighed and swallowed and put his hands over his face.

After a short while someone laid a hand on his shoulder. A woman's voice said, 'Are you in trouble?'

He gulped and breathed in. 'I'm at the end,' he told her.

'We're never at the end,' she said. 'You tell me about it.'

He told her everything. He started to talk long before he had taken a look at her and seen how lovely she was, and with what sympathy she listened to everything – not just the death of Carmen back in his college days, but even before that: his family, and never being able to do anything right or get anywhere in life.

She listened to the whole recital with interest and understanding. He couldn't believe there were still people in the world who were nice like that – who would come up and try to help you and not be sure that you'd turn out to be a maniac or a bore or a swindler.

Her name was Nancy. She told him that he had suffered so much because he had tried to live a lie, and that God wanted to give him the chance to live with the truth and to be a free man. When he was free, he would be happy.

Herb wondered how many of the others had told someone, and who it had been. Maybe they had told more than one person. For him, once had been enough: it had relieved the pressure, and after that the memory moved away from him so quickly that though the facts were still there, he thought about the episode as if it had been something he'd once seen on television. He no longer had any sense that it had happened to him; it might even have been someone else's story told to him in a bar somewhere, but with such vividness and detail that he could imagine it was his own story.

He had told his first wife, Elaine. He hadn't mentioned his fear or guilt or the sense of shame and remorse that had come over him later; nor had he said anything about the occasional patches of dread he went through when he began to feel that some day everything was going to catch up with him. He gave her an unadorned but biased account and she had said what he had hoped to hear: that it was an accident and he shouldn't brood about it; he was being too conscientious, too good. She made him think that nothing bad would develop from the death because he didn't deserve to have bad things happen to him.

He hadn't stressed the danger he had felt himself to be in. And he didn't think any of the others – if they had talked – would have. That was an important point. Divorced wives could be vicious about not getting their alimony on time. It was possible, for example, that while not exactly blackmailing a man, you could let him know that you still remembered something he'd told you. Dave's first wife might be like that, or Joe's – except that Joe wouldn't have told a wife; it would have been more likely for him to tell a friend from his combat unit. And Sherman, dearly as he loved the wife he'd stayed with all these years, would probably have chosen one of his brothers, or a cousin.

So far, there had been no consequences. And if Bill went to the police now, the four of them could get together and say he'd always been crazy, or they could tell the truth and say it was an unpleasant accident. He didn't really think they'd be put in jail. Their youth, drunkenness and shock would be taken into account, as well as the fact that all of them had led respectable lives afterwards and had families to protect. Bill was the only one who didn't have children.

He didn't think the worst would happen, but it was just as well to look ahead. Dave, he thought, would do anything to avoid publicity. He was an advertising man, who knew the value of appearances; he lived by them. A spell behind bars would be the end of him. He might not take any action himself, but he'd back up anyone else who did.

Joe was the one to watch. He could be likeable and charming, he could be a good friend. But he was stupid in so many different ways that you had to spend a lot of time putting things to him all dressed up, so that he wouldn't take offence or think you meant something else, or just get mad. He was also violent and his stint in the marines, when he was actually killing people every day as a job, hadn't driven the violence out of his system, only turned it into a routine.

When he thought about Joe, it seemed to Herb that he wouldn't be able to predict what would happen, even though he knew that Joe had a fear, a real mania, about being imprisoned or captured or in any way physically constrained. On the other hand, he did know about Sherman. Sherman, if he had to, would face the music. He wasn't really afraid of scandal or what other people thought. His family was right at the top. They could do just about anything and come out of it still admired. People would think he'd kept quiet only to save the others. No one would think badly of Sherman. Herb himself had always looked up to him, and still did.

Sherman would never raise his own hand against Bill. But would he allow somebody else to? That was going to be a tricky point. They had all heard Joe talk about killing. Not all of them would have taken it seriously. Herb did. He knew that Joe meant it, and would do it. And afterwards? Could you count on someone who was so ready to kill? And could you be sure that Sherman or even Dave might not go to the police? Whatever happened now, it wouldn't be the same as a drunken brawl.

As far as Herb was concerned, there had been a point after which the line was drawn and he decided: it must never be known that he was implicated in Carmen's death, or had even known anything about it. That point had come very early, at the moment when Carmen's uncle, Earl, had shaken his hand. He didn't understand why he felt so strongly, or what had happened to him at the time; but he knew that he wouldn't go back on that handshake. He had to be, for ever afterwards, a man who was believed to be innocent.

He took his wife, Sue, out to dinner and talked about plans for the summer – what the children wanted to do, whether they'd visit her mother at the end of June or in September. The night was cool, though a warm spell had been promised. In another couple of months it would be coming up to nineteen years since Carmen had gone over the roof.

She said, 'Everything in the garden's late this year. I'm sure it's making people depressed.'

'Who's depressed?'

'Just about everybody I know except you. The weather's so important, even for people who aren't farmers or gardeners. There's a lot of truth in that biological clock theory.'

'Keep winding it up every day?'

'You know what I mean. It's important to our state of mind. Light and dark, when we feel good, when we feel scared.'

'But not so important as other things.'

'Well, it's basic.'

'The weather can be overcome. Unless you're making your

living out of something that depends on it. It's less important to your moods than a good meal or a drink, or being with people you like, or having a broken arm or noisy neighbours, or feeling crowded, or—'

'All right, Herb,' she said. 'I'm not taking it to the Supreme Court.'

It was his turn to drive the babysitter home. Her name was Cheryl and she paid him the great compliment of removing her Walkman earphones in the car; when Sue was driving, she kept them on. Between themselves, they called her Miss Sunshine, because she always looked so miserable. She seemed half asleep too, but if you could get her to talk to you, she usually had something intelligent to say.

He said, 'Seen any movies lately?'

'A couple.'

He asked her about them. She'd seen a science-fiction fable for children, a weepie comedy-drama about charming kooks, and a story about lust and adultery which he knew she was too young to have been allowed to see.

'I saw that one too,' he said. 'I guess that was a pretty good plot for a perfect murder.'

'But they get her in the end. I didn't like that. I thought she was so smart she should have gotten away with it.'

'Well, she escaped to – wherever it was. A different country.'

'They get her with an extradition order. They can do that for murder.'

'Don't be too sure. She had all that money. She could buy her way out.'

'Maybe. I didn't think of that.'

'Does that make you feel better about it?'

She laughed. 'It's only a story,' she said. 'I just get mad when I keep seeing all this stuff on TV and everyplace where the women are always getting punished for practically breathing.'

'Is this Women's Lib or a desire for poetic justice?'

'Poetic justice is the other way around. That's when they don't get away with it.'

'Is it? I thought it meant happy endings. How would you commit the perfect murder?'

'I wouldn't plan it out too carefully.'

'Why not?'

'You plan it too much, and if something goes wrong, the plan isn't any good, so what you should do is forget about it and do it some other time. But what everybody does is: they go ahead with the busted plan. Then something else in it goes wrong and finally it's a mess, the whole thing, and you're stuck with it.'

'So how would you do it the right way?'

'That depends on whether I'd be a suspect or not. It's hard to murder anybody who's in your family, or an enemy, or a husband or wife.'

'I guess so.'

'Or if you'd gain from it – you know, if they'd left you something in their will.'

'I guess it would be safer to be alone, too. Or for nobody to suspect you had a connection with the other person.'

'Oh, you'd have to be on your own. Of course. And also, you'd have to choose your method.'

'Like what?'

'Make it look like an accident. That's the best way.'

'But not always easy to get an opportunity if you don't live with the person.' He turned the car in to the street where she lived and stopped outside the house. 'So, how would you do it?'

'I'd follow them around, and the first minute nobody was looking, I'd just run up and biff them over the head with a brick or something.'

'That could take years,' he said.

It could take a long time, and before you even started, you'd have to be willing to kill. Could he really do it? It had been bad enough the first time, when he hadn't actually been guilty of plotting a death, only of what was called manslaughter. This time, if he did anything, it would be murder. But, in his opinion, it would also be self-defence.

Dave picked Herb up on the street corner. It was raining lightly. As Herb got into the car, Dave said, 'OK?'

'All set.' Herb slammed the door. They moved off. 'What about the place?'

'It's perfect, completely isolated. The builders finished last week. It's already bought. All the furniture's there, kitchen working, pipes hooked up, the whole deal. Two of the houses are still unsold, but they're way at the other side. Anybody who wants to look at them has to go with somebody from the firm.'

'That's the kind of brother to have.'

'He thought first of all I wanted it to fix something up with a girl.'

'You need a whole house for that?'

'I got some food and liquor.'

'Fine. You tell us how much it was, and we'll pay our share.'

'This is on me,' Dave told him. 'I put it down on the squeeze-sheet, anyway.'

It started to rain heavily. Herb wiped the palms of his hands over his thighs. He said, 'Have you seen them yet?'

'No. Sherman's bringing them.'

'He knows the way OK?'

'We all did some dry runs the past few days. That's all right. The only thing I'm nervous about is Joe. He's going crazy. He wanted to go get them straight off the plane. He's afraid they'll talk to somebody.'

'We're the ones they want to talk to. They want to tell us why it's going to be good for our souls to do time in the State Pen. Jesus.'

'I kept telling him: they could have talked to hundreds of people before they left their place. They could have told their whole religious club.'

'And maybe they did. But I doubt that they'd give last names.'

'They could look up the register of who was rooming in the same house with him Sophomore year.'

'Well, what do you think?'

'I think we're going to have to stop them.'

'And how do we do that?'

'If it's necessary, an accident.'

'That's what everybody always says. I've been going around in circles trying to come up with some idea. Seems to me that's the hardest way to do it. What kind of accident did you have in mind?'

'Car crash?'

'How?'

'They rent a car—'

'They aren't going to need one. But say we could talk them into it, then we've got the Hertz people and the insurance and everybody in on it. Police experts measuring the tyre marks. That's no good.'

'I don't know why we're talking like this. I'm sure we can

persuade them. Especially the girl. She's bound to understand how it would affect the children.'

Herb opened his side window a notch and wiped the back of his hand down the windshield, where the glass was misting up. He said, 'You're right, it's no use talking about it.'

The other cars were waiting for them by the entrance of the estate. Dave honked his horn as they approached. He turned off on to the newly tarred drive. At the gatehouse he let down his window, leaned out and said to the guard inside, 'Hi, Charlie. It's OK.' Charlie waved his hand. The three cars moved on, coming to the end of the hard surface in the middle of a pine grove and reaching the old rocky dirt road, muddy from all the rain. They went slowly.

Dave pulled up outside the front walk of the house. Tall pine trees, which the architects had insisted on preserving, screened the other houses from them. The front lawn had been seeded with grass that was already growing. There were several bushes dotted around the brick walk.

They got out of the cars and raced for the house through the downpour. Dave unlocked the door with his keys and held it open for the others.

Everything was there: welcome mat outside, one inside to wipe your feet on, a stand for umbrellas, curtains on all the windows, new rugs wall-to-wall, lights and lamps, tables and chests of drawers, chairs and sofas covered in materials chosen to match the rugs and curtains.

Dave took the coats and said, 'Go on in and sit down. Sherman, get everybody a drink.'

'Gee, this is nice,' the girl said. Herb looked at Joe, who had his face bent over the coat he was handing to Dave; he looked as if he were trying to concentrate on something different from his surroundings, trying to remember a phone number or repeating something to himself.

Dave went into the kitchen. The rest of them entered the living room. Sherman introduced everyone. He started with Joe, who put his hands in his pockets and said, 'Hi, Bill.'

The girl stuck out her hand to be taken by him. Joe ignored it.

'This is my wife, Nancy,' Bill said. 'Aren't you going to shake hands?'

'What for? You're the ones planning to send me to jail, aren't you? That's going to be fun. A lot of fun for my wife and kids, too.'

'Oh, I don't think it'll come to that,' the girl said. 'And if it did, it wouldn't be for very long.' She had a flutey, pleading voice that went with her appearance: very thin, pale, with thin, mousy hair parted in the middle and dripping down her back; a narrow, almost noseless white face and eyes so light that the blue or grey seemed nearer to white. She looked undernourished, almost ill; or, if you wanted to think of it that way, ethereal. The expression on her face was sweet and enthusiastic, although not relaxed. She stood in a nervous way, too. Joe disregarded her. He walked into the kitchen by the other door.

Herb stepped forward. 'Hello, Bill,' he said. 'It's been a long time.' He held out his hand, knowing what he was doing. He'd thought about it ahead of time and he didn't mind.

'Sure has,' Bill said. He took Herb's hand in a dry, desperate grip. 'My wife, Nancy,' he added.

Herb shook her hand, too. It was cold, reminding him of his first wife, who had always had cold hands, even – like this – in the spring; it was probably a matter of poor circulation. But she also failed to give any kind of returning pressure. She offered him the limp hand like a dead fish, and then tried to remove it quickly. He let her go, but smiled. He'd been careful not to hold on too hard. She returned the smile beatifically. He was puzzled. Most of the newly converted people he'd met went out of their way to pump everyone's hand like politicians. She had the fervour, all right, but she appeared to be averse to physical contact. He wondered if she was really, seriously, ill.

'And a new wife,' he said. 'A lot of water under the bridge.'

Bill rose on his toes a couple of times and grinned. 'Best thing ever happened to me,' he said. He must have gone grey very early. He looked at least ten years older than the rest of them, and thin, and fairly bloodless, although nothing like his wife. That was what a clear conscience did for you. Or maybe, Herb thought, they were on some kind of religious diet.

Dave came in from the kitchen, followed by Joe. They were both carrying trays. Dave nodded, said, 'Hi, Bill. Hi, Nancy,' and looked for a place to set things down. 'What'll you have?' he asked.

'We don't drink alcohol,' Nancy said. 'Do you have any mineral water?'

'Tonic water.'

'That's artificially sweetened, and it contains drugs.'

'Drugs?'

'Quinine. Maybe just plain water.'

'We've got tomato juice.'

'That's got additives, too. It's artificial.'

'Just plain, ordinary water out of the faucet?'

'That'll be fine,' she said.

'Ice?' Dave asked. He was smiling a special, polite smile he used for idiots. Herb wondered if Bill would remember it. Probably not; he was beaming at the girl like a man who'd been hypnotized.

She did her own welcome smile back and said yes, please, ice would be wonderful. Joe's eyes flicked over to Herb; he looked as if he'd had a couple of stiff drinks out in the kitchen. So did Dave. Both of them were building up for an outburst or something – anger or laughter.

'Well, let's sit down,' Sherman said. He mixed drinks for himself and Herb and sat in a comfortable chair that stood a little way removed from the surrounding furniture.

Herb said, 'Well, it's nice of you two to come on out and get acquainted, let us talk everything over, put our point of view.'

Nancy and Bill simpered. She turned to Dave and asked, 'Where's your wife?'

'She's at the old house. I thought Sherm said: we haven't even moved in yet. It's going to take a couple more months still. I've just been using the place for entertaining clients, till we get organized.'

'Oh,' she said. She leaned forward and clasped her knees.

'You want to meet our families?' Joe yelled. 'Jesus Christ. Isn't it enough for you, you got us by the balls – you want to put the rest of them through it, too?'

The girl went grey. Herb, Sherman and Dave shouted at Joe.

He didn't pay any attention. 'Me shut up?' he went on. 'Why the hell should I?'

Herb stood up. 'Joe,' he ordered. 'Just go sit it out in the kitchen for a while, will you?' He crossed the room and put his hand on Joe's shoulder. Nobody spoke. 'Come on,' Herb whispered. Joe stood up. They went into the kitchen together.

Herb held a finger to his lips. They could hear Sherman smoothing things over behind them. Herb pulled Joe over to a counter lined with stools. He pushed him down on one of the straw-woven seats.

'We aren't going to win against that one,' Joe whispered. 'I recognize the type. Power trip. She's got this thing in her head like a rear end, that just won't give up. Look at her: no tits, no ass – he's the one guy she could get. Old enough to be her father, too. Religion, my foot. She's just another ballbreaker, that's all.'

'OK, OK,' Herb said.

'Listen, you give me the word and I'm ready to do it, right now. Just go in there and chop them both.'

'Let's see what we can do by talking,' Herb said.

'Oh, nobody ever—'

'Hang on. Wait. We don't know yet. This may be a blind. They may be planning to hit us for a little loan, right? Wait till we know. If it's no good, I'm with you. I'm only worried about making it look good. We've got to be able to explain everything afterwards.'

'Screw that. Knock them out, take them home to my place, cut 'em up with a power saw and feed the pieces into the disposal, burn the bones in the back yard.'

'I guess Cathy's going to love that.'

'I'll fix Cathy.'

'We've got to plan it.'

'You all are so worried about plans,' Joe hissed, 'you're never going to do it. Let's do it first and worry about it afterwards, for Christ's sake.'

'We'll see,' Herb told him. 'You stay here for a while.'

He went back into the living room. Dave was talking about how the city had changed since their college days.

They all looked up. Herb took his drink from the table and sat back down. He said, 'I guess you must have thought about this before you came. You don't have a family yet, but we do. All of us. We haven't told our wives. And we don't want to. It was only an accident, after all.'

'We killed him,' Bill said. 'You can't get away from that. I tried for years to forget about it, but it wasn't any good. I don't understand how you can feel this way: just – let it go, think it was something trivial. That boy died, and we killed him. It was a terrible thing. I know now that it was the most important event in my life.'

'But not in ours, Bill,' Sherman said. 'Herb's right. It was an accident.'

'Maybe on the surface. But if it was really so accidental, why didn't we go to the police afterwards?'

'Because that would have been extremely unpleasant for us and for everyone connected with us; and we thought we could get away with not having to.'

'And we were right,' Dave added, 'until you changed your mind.'

'It was a change of mind and a change of heart, too. I kept having that dream again, falling.'

'That was a metaphor,' Nancy said delicately, 'for sin.'

'I kept remembering, too. That night. It was a beautiful night. Trying to keep him from hitting us, holding him tight. He didn't have any clothes on. All that noise from Rockwell's. And the smell of the trees, leaves.'

'And you were drunk out of your mind,' Dave said.

'I was so drunk I was ready to do anything. Really excited, and I hated him. I was ready to throw him over. I wanted to.'

'You were giggling drunk,' Herb said, 'and then crying drunk. You weren't doing much of anything at all, either to help or to harm.'

'It was a long time before I knew what a horrible thing it was. Then I felt pity. A young life like that.'

'In the abstract,' Dave said. 'In the particular, he was a son of a bitch and we all thought so.'

Joe came in from the kitchen and sat on the arm of the sofa opposite Bill and Nancy.

'It wasn't right,' Bill said. 'I had the feelings of a murderer.'

'But not the deed,' Sherman told him.

'I also had an erection. That made it worse.'

'He remembers', Joe said, 'every time he gets one. That must have been a red-letter day. Dear Diary: guess what happened today?'

'Joe?' Sherman said.

'We got to listen to this? He just wants to keep confessing till he runs out of listeners. He isn't going to be happy till it's in the papers. Public confession. You'll see. Just wait.'

'We killed him,' Bill said.

Nancy put a hand on his arm and said, 'He's right. You know he is.'

'How old are you?' Herb asked.

'Twenty-two,' she said.

'And you don't have children. But we do. Think of our children.'

Her face became transformed, as though something had been poured into it. 'That's just what I'm thinking about,' she told him.

Bill said, 'Nancy's had more experience with children than any of you. She used to teach handicapped kids.'

'Now she's stuck on handicapped grown-ups,' Joe said.

'How would you like', she asked Herb, 'those poor children to know their daddies were murderers?'

'It wasn't murder,' Dave said. 'Quit using that word. It was an accident. And nobody's going to know about it unless you tell.'

'And', Herb added, 'their suffering would be on your head. You'd be responsible for it. Why would you want to bring that on our families? If you don't tell, they won't know.'

'When you tell the truth,' she said, 'they'll know you were big enough to own up.'

Joe threw his glass across the room. It hit the side of the coffee table with a loud crack. Bill and Nancy recoiled into the cushions.

Joe shouted, 'Oh, you dumb namby-pamby bitch!'

Bill jumped up. 'You always did hate women,' he said, 'and anybody that had decent feelings. Anybody who's even slightly above your level.'

Dave and Herb started to haul Joe out into the kitchen again. 'It makes me sick,' he said as they pulled him along. 'You're going to tell me what's good for me while you ruin my life. To make you feel the truth's been told and everything's all nice and clean now, you bastards.'

Bill called after them, 'You always were an oaf.' He sat back down and put his arm around Nancy.

She said to Sherman, 'I think we'd better be going soon.'

'So do I,' he said, 'but let's give it about fifteen minutes more. We'll talk about something else while they straighten themselves out, out there. Don't be too hard on Joe. He went through a pretty hard time in Vietnam.'

'He was always like that,' Bill said.

'I don't think so. He was very good to his family. He worked hard all through college, remember? And kept sending money home to help his mother and sister. He's a little unruly, but not as bad as you think.'

'He was always like this,' Bill repeated primly. 'A violent man.'

'We're all violent, Bill.'

'No.'

'Yes. We try to keep it reined in, that's all. To control it, and to put it to use. It's energy, and energy can be a good thing. All the vices can be used. Greed, for instance – greed can build a prosperous land out of nothing but forests and plains. It's the making of any frontier country.'

'I don't know what you're talking about.'

'I'm talking about tolerance. I think you should let other people lead their lives according to their own standards.'

'We killed him. Whether it was conscious and deliberate or subconsciously desired and not admitted – that doesn't matter. Either way, he's dead.'

'Of course it matters,' Sherman said. 'They're two entirely different things. Even the law distinguishes between kinds and degrees of motive.'

'But does God?' Nancy asked.

'Well, as to that, God's got a tougher job. He's supposed to forgive everybody everything.'

'Only if you repent,' she said. She hitched herself forward eagerly. Once more her face became transfigured by the intensity of her beliefs. She said, 'I know you're all afraid, but you don't realize – there isn't anything to fear. This is going to be a good thing. It isn't going to be easy, but when it's over, you'll be clean. You'll be free.'

'We'll be in jail. We're free now.'

'I mean, in your hearts. Better a free man in jail than a guilty one outside. Bill knows that.'

'But Bill was that way before the accident.'

'What?'

'How's that?' Bill said.

'You reacted that way because you brought it with you. When Carmen died, that just gave you something to pin it all on to. You know what I'm talking about.'

'But I've straightened all that out now. And she's right. You can't be free if you're living a lie. I know you're scared of the publicity and all that. But the truth is more important.'

'To whom?'

'To God,' Nancy said.

'Well, God knows the truth already, and if you'll forgive me saying so, God isn't going to get thrown in the slammer and neither are you. The rest of us are in a better position to talk about how we feel about truth.'

'God—'

'That's another thing. The god you keep talking about is your god, isn't that right? It might not be mine.'

'Oh, He would be,' she pleaded, 'if only you'd open your heart to Him.' She held out her arms in a stagey gesture. She looked half-demented.

Sherman said, 'That's going to take a lot longer than fifteen minutes.'

'We'll stay,' she said. 'We've got all the time in the world for that. That's the truly important part. What does life hold for any of us, without the spiritual side?'

In the kitchen Herb moved the bottle away from Joe. Dave lit a cigarette and said, 'I can't do anything against a girl like that. She's so frail and helpless. She's like a child. I hadn't expected her to be so pretty.'

Joe snorted. 'That whiney, rabbit-faced woman – you call that pretty?'

'Are we going to go to jail for the rest of our lives', Herb asked, 'because she's pretty?'

'It won't come to that.'

'Near enough. Whatever it comes to, they're both in it together.'

'I couldn't.'

'It's up to you, Dave. You know what it means if we don't stop them.'

'If we all go to the police together—'

'Jesus, are you dumb,' Joe said. 'We aren't going to get away with this till we've been washed in the blood of the lamb and had the baptism of fire and all the rest of that crap. She's off her head. And she's got him right where she wants him.'

Dave shook his head.

'I know what you mean,' Herb told him. 'I actually think she's the best thing that ever happened to him, like he said, only it's extremely unfortunate that we all have to get dragged in, too. She should have been willing to stick with just one.'

'I can do it,' Joe said. 'I can do it tonight and I can do it right now. I've got everything.'

'What?' Dave said.

'Knives, monkey wrench, couple of guns I brought back.'

'No.'

Herb said, 'Dave, if you and Sherm could hold the fort here for a couple of hours, we'll take Bill and Nancy for a little sightseeing.'

'In the rain? In the dark?'

Joe smiled.

'You don't have to do anything,' Herb said. 'Just keep Sherman happy. Get him to talk about their trip to Hong Kong.' He stood up. 'You go back first. I want a word with Joe.'

Dave looked at his cigarette. He took three quick puffs, a long drag, and stubbed out what was left. He got up and went into the living room.

Herb stared at the door for a moment.

Joe said, 'OK. How do you want me to do it?'

'Do you have a shovel?'

'Two. We knock them out, beat up the faces, take off the fingertips.'

'Afterwards – what do we do about checking them out of their hotel, packing up their stuff, and so on?'

'We go in and pack it all up, take it away. Don't bother to check them out. We could be recognized later. Let the hotel think they've been bilked.'

'We shouldn't have put them in a hotel in the first place. I didn't think.'

'It doesn't matter. Main thing is, to do something about it. Not tomorrow: tonight. Now.'

Herb hesitated. He had drunk enough to be confident about carrying out any scheme successfully, but he had also reached the stage where he thought he was having important revelations about life, becoming aware of things he'd never thought of before. He understood, for instance, for the first time that what had been so hard for Joe about the war was coming back to a place where he'd no longer be able to kill. He'd been trained for it, it was something he was good at, and suddenly nobody would let him do it. Or maybe he had killed people. Who could tell? There were always unsolved crimes. Joe seemed easy and relaxed now; now that he'd made his decision, he was looking forward to carrying it out.

Herb realized that he was breathing too quickly and sweating a lot. He thought that even if the whole plan went without a hitch, Joe couldn't be trusted. Because if he was the one to do the killing, he'd know that the others could give him away. And he'd wonder if they were asking themselves about him. Could you ever depend on a killer?

He felt his insides winding up tighter and tighter. There was no way to avoid what was coming. 'OK,' he said. 'Count me in.'

'Right. You drive left, go all the way down the side behind the houses that aren't finished yet. There isn't anybody around now. You drive into the woods there and stop when I tell you.'

They went back to the living room, where Dave was talking about deafness, speech impediments and the parents of what Bill was calling 'disadvantaged' children. He stopped when the others looked towards the door.

Herb said, 'Well, it's getting late now and there's still a lot to talk about. I'd really appreciate it if you could come back tomorrow and continue the discussion. I sort of feel maybe we should get our families in on it, too.'

'I think that would be a very good idea,' Nancy said fervently. 'I've thought that right from the beginning.'

'Yes,' Bill said.

'Right. Joe and I can take you back to town. Sherm and Dave, if you could clear up here, we'll see you later.'

Everyone stood up. Joe was the only one who didn't say anything. Nancy and Bill didn't appear to like the idea of getting into a car with him, but the fact that Herb was there too seemed to make it all right.

'Well,' Nancy said. 'Well, it's been nice meeting you. I'll look forward to our next discussion.'

Herb drove. Nancy and Bill sat in the front seat with him, Nancy on the outside. Joe was in the back.

The rain had eased off to a light drizzle. Herb took the path to the side and drove as Joe had directed.

'Is this the way we came in?' Bill asked.

'No,' Herb said. 'This way's supposed to get us out on to a quicker way home.' He kept going until the car wallowed through the mud into a clearing.

'OK, Herb,' Joe said.

He stopped the car, keeping the lights on and the windshield wipers working.

Joe leaned forward over Bill's neck. 'Out,' he said. 'We're going to talk some more.'

Bill said, 'No, we've talked enough.' His voice was quavery.

Joe said, 'Son of a bitch,' and there was an explosion that threw Herb against the door. It took him a moment to realize that Joe had shot Bill in the back of the head. The bullet had gone through, drilling a hole in the safety glass in front and spraying blood and brains all over the inside of the car. The smell was like something out of a cage in the zoo. Herb opened his door and tumbled into the rain and fresh air. Nancy, on the other side, was screaming and trying to get her door open.

It wasn't what they had planned. The agreement had been for Joe to get the two out at gunpoint while Herb brought the shovels from the trunk; to threaten them with the gun in order to make them dig, and then afterwards shoot one apiece, dump them in, and cover them up. If they wouldn't both dig, Joe would threaten Nancy, to make Bill do the work, and Herb would take the second shovel.

'You want out?' he heard Joe saying. 'OK, sweetheart.'

Herb leaned over the hood of the car. He thought he was going to be sick. He could hear the two of them fighting, Joe beating her across the face with the pistol barrel while she tried to kick him and break free. Then there was a clunk as the gun was put down on the car, next to Herb's head.

He looked up. One of the headlights blazed into the rows of pine trees. The light from the other one came and went as Joe forced Nancy across the front bumper. He hit her in the face again twice and started to rip her clothes away. He shrieked at her, 'This is going to be the best thing that ever happened to you.'

Herb watched, dazed, as Joe tore off her skirt and slip and, still yelling at her, began to pull at her tights and underpants. Her arms made tentative pushing motions like those of a child in sleep, but she was barely trying to defend herself. She moved her blood-smeared face jerkily from side to side. Herb thought as he caught sight of her misshapen profile that her lips must be cut, her nose and some of her teeth broken. He reached for the pistol by his hand, felt that the safety catch was on, pushed it up, and held the barrel to Joe's forehead. Joe didn't look up;

he called out, 'Piss off – you can have her next.' Herb pulled the trigger.

It was just like the movies, only louder. Joe spun backwards and down to the side and Nancy collapsed on top of him, whimpering.

He checked the gun. He put it inside the car on the front seat. He went around to the opposite side and got hold of Joe, dragging him to where he could heave him into the back seat. When he returned for Nancy, she hadn't moved. Her skirt and slip were lying in the mud. The coat she was still wearing was streaked and sodden. He shook out the skirt and slip, took them back to the car and started to clean up the inside of the windshield with them. Then he went back to get her.

He pushed her into the back with Joe, got into the front seat, turned around, and put the gun to her head. She opened her eyes and stopped crying. She said in an almost voiceless screech, 'I'll never tell. Let me go and I'll never tell, so help me.'

Of course she'd tell. She had started the whole business because all her thoughts had to be referred to an outside agency. She was incapable of judging a thing according to itself, only according to the rulebook, to the instructions her god was supposed to have laid down about the conduct of human affairs. She had never killed anybody – she just forced other people to kill. If he let her go, it would happen all over again. He shot her without thinking twice about it.

He drove back to the part of the site where their house was. It was the only one that had any lights on. He stopped for a minute to try to figure out what he should do first and whether he should drive home in Dave's car, whether he'd have to kill the security man at the entrance, whether he could walk back to town.

He decided to go back in Dave's car and take a chance that the man at the gate would recognize the car, and not him.

There was no other way he could cover himself. He had to have one of the cars to get back – that was certain. What else? He had to be safe afterwards. Sherman: he could count on Sherman, but not on Dave. There were three dead people now, and no way to stop Dave yelling about it. Herb could hear how it would sound: *I had nothing to do with this. I don't want any part of it.* He, Herb, would be standing there covered in mud, rain and blood, and the perfect person to take responsibility for everything, past and present.

But, if he did anything to Dave, Sherman wouldn't stand for it.

He started the car up again and drove it slowly forward, cut the engine, got out and let it roll down the incline towards the front of the house. He took the pistol with him and let himself in the front door.

He went through the hall, into the living room. Dave jumped up, saying, 'Jesus, Herb. You scared me.'

Herb circled around to the back of Sherman's chair. Sherman was his friend, the one he'd always liked best. He put the pistol to the back of Sherman's head and, as Sherman was about to turn, fired.

Dave screamed, 'Herb, what are you doing? What are you doing?'

Herb said, 'I can't figure out any other way, Dave.' He came closer. He couldn't remember how many bullets ought to be left and he couldn't afford to miss. Dave was still too shocked to move away. He'd stood up, that was all. He had one hand on the arm of his chair. The other still held his glass and a cigarette.

Herb walked straight up to him. He said, 'Just stay that way for a minute', as if he were a photographer, put the pistol against Dave's temple, and squeezed the trigger.

After that, he went crazy. He knew he had to hurry before anyone came, before he could be caught. He panted and talked to himself, his teeth chattered. He worried about all the noise there had been.

He threw the patio doors wide and drove both cars into the living room, took the other keys from Dave's pocket, wiped his prints off the steering wheels and anything else he could remember touching, poured gasolene all over the rug and furniture and bodies, and spent nearly five minutes looking for Dave's cigarette lighter, which he finally found in the kitchen.

Everything looked ready. His eyes went around the living room, around and around. It looked all right.

He opened the front door, flicked on the flame, and threw the lighter into the room. Then he slammed the door and ran.

He was behind the wheel of the car and driving away within seconds. The light came up in the driving mirror and he could hear the glass go from the windows of the house. The place would burn for hours. And it probably hadn't yet been connected to any kind of alarm system.

The road going out was even worse than when they'd driven in. He approached the entrance booth cautiously. As far as he could see, the guard was still in his box; no warning had gone through. But the man wanted to talk to him. Herb pretended that he hadn't seen; he raised his hand in greeting, eased the car forward, then lowered his head and stepped on the gas.

The wheels gripped on the gravel beneath the mud and shot him ahead. He raced the car down to the highway and kept going for a long time at top speed. There was no one else around. He dodged down a few side lanes and made his way back to town by a different route. He was surprised at how well he remembered the old roads from his college days. He remembered lots of things from those times as he drove; they seemed to have come from someone else's life, not from his.

He parked the car in town, wiped the wheel, and examined his face in the mirror. He took the subway back to his hotel for a shave and a shower, checked out, got a cab to the airport and left for home.

On the plane he sat next to a girl who had brought two tennis racquets with her, which she'd stowed away in one of the top compartments. She kept asking Herb to get up, so she could see that no one put any heavy briefcases on top of them.

'You want the aisle seat?' he asked.

'If you don't mind.'

'It's fine by me, but I think it's OK now. We're all packed up.'

She said, 'It's just so easy to damage them and it costs a lot to have them restrung. And they're never the same afterwards, no matter what they tell you. It's like putting new soles on a pair of shoes – it never works. They don't feel right. Not to me, anyway.'

'Are you going to play in the tournaments?' he asked.

'No, just people to people.'

'That can be the most dangerous kind.'

'Why?'

'No rules.'

She laughed. The rules, she said, were the same for amateurs as for professionals. 'The only difference is that you're with your friends. And with your friends – well, you know where you are, don't you?'

'Exactly,' he said.

Third Time Lucky

Lily had married first when she was eighteen. He'd been killed in Vietnam. She'd married again when she was twenty-one. He too had died in Vietnam. She'd had proposals after that, but she'd refused without even considering the possibility of accepting. She was sure that if she said yes, he'd be killed just as the first two had been. It was like having a curse on you: she could feel it. Perhaps when she'd agreed to go to the Egyptian exhibition she'd been attracted by the knowledge that there was something called the Curse of The Pharaohs.

She'd forgotten all about that. She didn't remember it again until long after she'd heard the radio interview with the old woman who lived in Cairo.

Lily listened to the radio a lot. As a child she'd been introduced to literature through the soap operas; even at the age of seven, she'd realized that the stories were preposterous, but she loved them. She'd also liked the way they gave you only a little piece of each story every day, so that if you were lucky enough to get sick, or if school had been cancelled because of snow, you could hear the complete collection from morning to late afternoon – like eating a whole meal of Lifesavers, all in different flavours.

In her teens she'd watched television, mainly the late-night movies. And then later, when the most popular family show had been the war, she'd stopped. She'd gone back to the radio. Her favourite station broadcast its programmes from the other side of the ocean in British voices that sounded just like the people in the movies. She was charmed by their accents.

The woman who lived in Egypt had spoken in one of a number of interviews compiled by an English woman reporter. The programmes set out to make a study of British people who had lived in Egypt for a long time. All the broadcasters were women: that, apparently, was the point of the series. One of the speakers was a girl who'd married an Egyptian; she talked about what it was like to become part of the family, how it was different from life at home, and so on: she seemed to have a very happy marriage. She could also throw in foreign phrases as easily as she spoke her own language, her voice full of enthusiasm. She praised her mother-in-law. Lily was drawn across the room as she listened: she went and sat right next to the radio to make sure she didn't miss anything or that she could retune if the speech broke up in static – a thing that often happened during the international programmes.

She was fascinated by accounts of other people's marriages. She couldn't hear enough. It was like being told fairytales, and yet it was the real thing – real people her own age. Once she'd grown up, she'd started to prefer fact to fiction. That was what she thought, anyway.

Immediately after the young married woman came an archaeologist. And after her, the reporter introduced the old woman.

Her name was Sadie. She'd been born and brought up in London. When she was six years old her father had taken her to the British Museum to look at the exhibits. There she had seen a room full of Egyptian mummies and had been so impressed by them that she couldn't sleep. She'd said to her parents that her home was in the place where those people had lived, and that was where she wanted to go, because that was where she belonged. Her parents had told her not to be silly. When she persisted, they called in a friend who wasn't exactly a doctor, but who knew a lot. The friend succeeded in restoring Sadie's sleep by assuring her that strange as her story sounded to everyone else, there might be something to it. She would be free to test the truth of it as soon as she grew up. But to insist on instant transportation to a distant country wouldn't be fair to her parents while they were still trying to give her a good home and make sure she was well-fed and healthy.

Sensible man, Lily thought. That was the kind of doctor people should have – not like the ones who'd tried to deal with her and who'd probably primed her mother with a load of nonsense until the whole family was driving her crazy. It had been as if twice in her life she'd become a freak – like a woman who'd been struck by lightning and survived. It was almost like going through the sort of thing she'd read about in magazine stories: accounts of women who'd had to keep on living in a community when everyone there knew they'd been the victims of some shameful act of violence or humiliation.

Of course people felt sorry for you and they hoped to make you well again. They believed that you ought to recover. They tried to cheer you up and yet they wanted you to be suffering the correct amount for the occasion, otherwise they got nervous: there might be some extra grief around that wasn't being taken care of. She herself had sometimes thought: *Am I feeling the right things? Am I even feeling enough?* She didn't know. She thought she didn't know much of anything any more.

She started hanging around the museum in order to fill up her days. She'd gone back to work, but there were lunch hours when she didn't want to be eating her sandwiches with the rest of the girls, and the museum wasn't far from the job she'd had at the time.

She began by just walking around. That first day she saw Greek statues and Roman coins. The second time she went, she looked at Chinese jade and Japanese scroll paintings. On her third visit she got lost trying to find the Etruscans, and came upon ancient Egypt instead. It hadn't produced an instant, revelatory obsession like the one experienced by the six-year-old Sadie, but it had certainly done something extraordinary to her. She had felt magnetized by the appearance of everything: the colours, the style of drawing, the mysterious hieroglyphics – the whole look. The museum had several items that were rare and important: a black wooden panther surmounted by a golden god in a high hat; a painted mummy case that was covered in pictures of birds, animals and pictograph writing; a grey stone hawk that stood about four feet high; and a granite statue of a seated Pharaoh who had a face framed by a head-dress that merged with the shoulders, so that he too had the silhouette of a hawk.

She knew then, at her first sight of the sculpture and painting, that she wanted to find out more about the people who had made them. She picked up a leaflet at the main desk. It turned out that there were museum lectures you could attend in the mornings or afternoons. There were even some that took place during the lunch hour. She signed up in a hurry.

Her real conversion to the art of Egypt happened in semi-darkness, to the accompaniment of a low hum given off by the museum's slide projector. She studied temples, frescoes, jewellery, furniture, corpses thousands of years old. She felt that all these sights and objects were familiar to her in a way that her own life was not.

The Englishwoman named Sadie hadn't needed lectures. After the family friend had made her see reason, she'd struck a bargain with her parents: that she'd be good and do what they told her, as long as they realized that her one ambition was to go to Egypt, and that she actually did plan to go there as soon as she was grown up. It took several more years, and undoubtedly a certain amount of research, before she narrowed down the rather vague passion for Egyptology to a specific dedication: she found out through a dream that in a former life she'd been a priestess of Isis and many centuries ago she had lived in a particular house, where she'd had a wonderful garden full of flowers and herbs, and plants that possessed healing properties. It became her mission to return to the house, live there and replant her garden.

It had taken Sadie twelve years of work in London to raise the money for her fare. On her arrival in Egypt she attached herself to British archaeological societies, which allowed her to earn a little by helping them, although – because she'd had so little formal schooling – they discounted anything she had to say on their subject. It came as a surprise to the official bodies when she discovered the ruins of what she insisted was her house, and which, as it was excavated, proved to have contained at one time a plentifully stocked courtyard garden. It was surprising, but not in anyone else's opinion a matter of supernatural or preternatural knowledge, as Sadie claimed. In spite of the scepticism of the experts, she managed to present the urgency of her desire so convincingly that she was given permission to camp out in the ruins and eventually to try to reconstruct the house and garden.

When the woman reporter interviewed her, Sadie was eighty-two. She spoke of the quest for her true home with an assurance and simplicity that made Lily think what a good life it had been: to know so exactly, from such an early age, what you wanted and where you belonged. If she herself had had that kind of vision as a child, she might now feel that her life meant something, instead of thinking that it all just seemed to be dribbling away around her, never getting anywhere, always going wrong.

Egypt had begun to be important to her for about a year and a half, yet she didn't recall the circumstances of her breakdown until she'd been going to the lectures for five weeks. The memory came back as if it had fallen on top of her. While she was looking at slides of famous statues and wall paintings, she recognized certain things that she'd seen when the great Tutankhamun exhibition had come over to America. That was shortly after she was supposed to have recovered from her second widowing. Friends and relatives had thought it would be a nice idea, a treat, to take her to the show. She didn't care what she went to see. She'd said sure, OK.

It was too long a trip to make all in one day, so she'd stayed with her aunt, and even then it was a considerable drive by car from there. Her cousin, Charlie, and his girlfriend, Sue, drove in one car, while two of Sue's old schoolfriends went in the second one, together with some friend of theirs – a man who, Lily suspected, had been asked along because of her. That too had happened after her first husband had died: everybody had started trying to match her up with somebody.

The lines of sightseers waiting to get in to see the exhibition had been so long, and so often mentioned in the papers, that everyone had a different theory about what was the best time to go, when to avoid the school groups, the adult education classes, the old, the young, the tourists. They got into the line in the middle of the afternoon, and were fortunate – they had to wait for only an hour and a quarter.

Lily took out her wallet to pay, but Charlie and Sue insisted on buying her ticket. She put the ticket into the change compartment of the wallet, on the side where she kept her backdoor key and her lucky-piece – an old silver coin covered in patterns that might have been foreign writing; a great-uncle had brought it back from overseas. The coin had been in the safe with the rest of her grandmother's treasured and worthless ornaments. Her father had given it to her because she'd seemed to be so interested in the markings on it.

The line advanced slowly, even after they had paid. The guards were being careful to let in only a certain number at a time. Nobody wanted to have overcrowding or pushing. And, naturally, the people who were already inside would feel they were entitled to stay there a good long while, after having waited so long, paid so much, and at last come face to face with objects of such magnificence.

Lily wasn't expecting to be asked for her ticket when a hand was suddenly held out to her. She scrabbled around quickly in her bag and found the stub as the crowd moved forward into the darkness.

All at once everyone fell silent. People were afraid of tripping over themselves in the dark, or bumping into each other. She fumbled in her wallet, shut the change purse, zipped up her bag and held on to it tightly. She was looking at a set of floodlit glass boxes that sprang from the darkness like lighted boats crossing an ocean at night. In each glass case a single treasure was positioned. The lighting must have been controlled from above, although it was impossible to see how. The impression was definitely that all the illumination emanated from the golden deities and blue animals, painted birds and flowers.

Lily stared and lost track of the time. There was no doubt in her mind that the jars, tables, gods, faces, jewels and masks were gazing back, looking out from the repose of their long past and giving something to her as she passed by.

She stopped in front of an alabaster vase shaped like a lotus blossom on its stem. The crowd jostled her lightly, but no one was shoving. The atmosphere seemed churchlike: the worshippers in darkness, the sacred relics shining. She lingered for a long time in front of a beautiful face – yellow-white, with black lines painted on the eyebrows, around the eyes and outward at the sides. The face was framed in a head-dress like the one worn by the sphinx. And the whole thing, according to the description underneath, was part of a canopic jar. She'd forgotten what canopic meant.

She stepped aside, to let other people see. In front of the cases of jewellery, a young man had come to a standstill; he'd apparently been in the same place for a long while, because an official was trying to get him to move. The young man responded immediately, saying – in a very audible voice – that he'd paid his money and he had a right to look for as long as he wanted to. The official backed away, murmuring about being fair to the other people: he didn't want to start a fight in the middle of the crowd or to disrupt the discreet, artistic and historic hush brought about by the presence of so many tons of gold and lapis lazuli.

She took a good look herself at the young king in his blue-

and-gold headcloth, which fell in stripes to his shoulders. And as she walked on, she realized that she'd worked her way around to the exit. The others were nearby. Sometimes people went through exhibits at such different rates that it made more sense to split up for a set period; but they'd all finished at about the same time.

They moved out into the shopping area where people were selling books and postcards. Lily opened her bag and got out her wallet. She unsnapped the coin compartment and began to rummage inside it. She couldn't feel her lucky-piece. She couldn't see it. She shook the bag from side to side. Sue asked what was wrong. Charlie said, 'If you're looking for your wallet, you're already holding it in your hand.'

The next thing she knew, she was screaming. Everyone tried to calm her down but she let go completely, shrieking hysterically, 'I've lost it, oh God. It isn't anywhere.'

'Something important?' a voice said.

'The most important thing I've got,' she spluttered. 'It's my lucky-piece.' She wanted to go back into the exhibition rooms, to make the museum authorities turn up the lights and hold the crowds back, so that she could go over the whole floor.

They couldn't do that, everyone told her. They'd report the loss and hope the staff would pick up the coin at closing-time.

That wasn't good enough, she yelled.

Shock, embarrassment, distaste, were on people's faces. She didn't care. She could barely see them but she could hear the change in the sounds around her, and especially the difference in their voices as they let her know that everything she wanted was impossible and unreasonable. They thought her lucky-piece was insignificant; she was in the presence of Art and of the past, and of an entire civilization that had been lost. She even heard one of their own crowd whispering about her – though later on she wasn't sure if she might not have imagined it – saying, 'Don't know why she wants it back – it didn't do her much good, did it?' All she knew was that losing the coin seemed to her the final blow. She'd lost everything else: she couldn't lose that, too.

The lucky-piece had had little worth as silver and no real value to anyone but her. Nevertheless, despite the efforts of the museum authorities and their cleaning crew, the coin never turned up. And she finally learned to accept its loss, as well as to understand that she'd had some sort of collapse, and that maybe she had needed to express her grief in that way, in public. She also realized – many months after the event – what she must have forgotten at the time: that all those wonderful objects they'd been admiring had been the contents of a grave.

And, eventually, it seemed to her that the loss of the lucky-piece had been a sign; it had been intended to happen, so that she would have no doubt about the fact that there was a curse on her. She had married two men and both of them had died. She was certain that if she tried to find happiness again, the same thing would happen a third time.

She didn't say anything about the curse to the men who took her out, courted her, and wanted to marry her or just to sleep with her. She merely said no. When Don Parker asked her to be his wife, she said no for four months, said maybe for two, and in the end told him she would if he'd take her to Egypt for the honeymoon.

'You don't know how lucky you are,' her mother said to her one evening. 'The chances you've had. They aren't going to keep asking for ever, you know.'

From across the room Lily gave her newspaper a shake. Her mother sewed a button on the wristband of a blouse. They were waiting for Channel Two to show the play. That week it was a repeat of an old one – Ingrid Bergman and Trevor Howard in *Hedda Gabler*. Lily read in her paper about an African bird called a hoopoe that had been closed up inside a packing crate by mistake and been found at a German airport; the authorities had trapped it in an airline hangar and were just about to catch it with a net – in order to send it back to its own country – when it flew into one of the wire-strengthened glass panes up near the ceiling and broke its neck.

She turned the page. The paper crinkled noisily. She held it high, the way her father did at the breakfast table. She read about floods, fires, insurrections, massacres and robberies. She read about a chemist in Florida who believed that the building-blocks of ancient Egypt's pyramids could have been poured into moulds rather than quarried.

Everything she saw now reminded her of Egypt. It was like following the clues in a detective story. It was like being in love. Once you were aware of a thing, a name, or a word, you began to notice it everywhere. And once you had seen the truth of one cause of pain, you could recognize others. It was only after her breakdown in the museum that she understood how little her mother liked her – in fact, that her mother had never loved her. Perhaps she'd never loved Lily's sister, Ida, either. Ida was married and had two children; her husband had divorced her. And now Ida and her mother and the two children – both girls – were locked in an insatiable battle of wills that everyone except Lily would probably have called familial love. To Lily it seemed to be an unending struggle invented by her mother because otherwise life would have no meaning. Lily's father hadn't been enough of a challenge. And Lily herself had escaped into the protection of the two tragic events that had isolated her from other people.

'There's a man down in Florida,' Lily said, 'who thinks the pyramids were poured.'

'Oh?' her mother answered. She wasn't interested. She probably thought it meant they'd been poured through a funnel.

'It could be true, I guess. There's been a lot about Egypt recently. There was the woman who believed she was the priestess of Isis. I told you about her. She went to live there.'

'Just another nut. She's like that woman who says she's receiving spirit messages from Mozart and Beethoven, and then she plays those cheap little things.'

'That isn't a very good example. She's such a nut, she's made millions – on TV and everything. But in her case, you really wonder if she's a fraud.'

'Are you kidding? Of course she is. You think Beethoven—'

'You wonder if she's tricking people deliberately, instead of just deceiving herself. Now, this other woman – well, what you wonder about that, is: could there actually be some deep, biological, hereditary impulse directing her? Something we don't know about yet. See what I mean? I read an article a few years ago that talked all about people's sense of direction; it said they've found out that we've all got this magnetic centre in the brain.'

'Oh, boy.'

'Well, that's what it said.'

'What does Don say when you come out with these things?'

'He said yes. I told him I'd marry him if he took me to Egypt for the honeymoon, so he said he would. He's getting the tickets this week.'

Her mother's face came up from the buttons and thread. 'What are you talking about?'

'We're getting married after New Year's,' Lily announced. 'I just said so.' Her mother looked astounded. 'I told you,' Lily repeated. 'When I said we were going to Egypt.'

'I didn't take it in,' her mother said. She stared.

'Well, that's the end of the news.'

'That means . . . the wedding, the invitations, the catering. Why does it have to be so soon?'

'That's the best time to go.'

'Go? Where?'

'To Egypt,' Lily snapped. 'Are you feeling all right? We're planning a quiet wedding, in a registry office. His mother's going to take care of the reception at that house they've got down in the country.'

'You don't know how lucky you are,' her mother said again.

And you resent that, Lily thought.

'To have a boy like that.'

It doesn't matter how nice people are, if you don't love them. You love him more than I do. To me, he's unexciting. I've been at parties where girls were flirting with him, and I've said to myself: well, they just don't know how dull he is. I've even been in a shop where the tie salesman obviously thought he was the nearest thing to a classical statue he'd ever come across. But not for me.

'So good-looking.'

So boring, and actually sometimes irritating. I couldn't last out a lifetime of it. I should never have gotten myself into this mess. But it's nice to be admired like that; it's flattering. And I can't go on living this way.

Her mother said, 'I guess that extra-sensory, reincarnation stuff started back in the twenties, when they found the tomb.'

'No. It began before that. It was part of the Victorian interest in psychic phenomena. It all had to do with the disintegration of Christianity.'

'Is that right?'

'That's what they told us in school.'

Her mother went back to her sewing. They didn't talk again. They hardly ever talked, anyway. Ida had always taken the brunt of her mother's blame, inquisitiveness, disapproval, worry and desire to interfere. Lily used to think that that showed a difference in the quality of her mother's love, though recently it had occurred to her that maybe it was simply a matter of positioning: that she had been in the wrong place at the wrong time, so that the only mother-love she could remember had come from her father, her grandfather, one aunt, and a cousin who was of her grandmother's generation. She knew how lucky she was about that: some people didn't have anyone at all.

She and Don had the vaccinations they needed, got the passports ready, and rushed out invitations. Lily had no time to go to the museum any more, but she began to have the same dream at night, often several times in the week: she found herself standing in sunlight, under a blue sky, and looking up at a huge, almost endlessly high sandstone wall above her; it was a golden-tan colour and carved all over with strange writings like hieroglyphics. In the dream she stood and looked at the picture-writing and couldn't figure out what it said. She guessed that the lines on her lucky-piece had been the same – they'd meant something, but no one knew what. She liked the dream. Very few dreams in her life had ever repeated; the ones that did were all landscape-dreams: just special places she remembered, that were good spots for nice dreams to start from. She'd never had a repeating dream that was a puzzle, but it pleased her to be standing in the sun, under the hot sky that was so blue and far away, and examining the foreign shapes of an unknown language. In real life, outside the dream and outside her apartment, the air was bitter, there was deep snow on the ground and more blizzards had been forecast. She hoped that the airlines wouldn't have to ground their planes for long. She was impatient to leave.

Two days before they were due to fly, they read and heard about a sandstorm that had closed all the airports in Egypt. The storm was actually a giant cloud. The papers and television said it stretched from Cairo to Israel. Lily became agitated. She thought they might not be able to take off. Don patted her arm and smiled at her. Ever since she'd accepted his proposal he'd been smiling inanely; it made her so guilty and annoyed that she almost wanted to hurt him in some way. She could feel herself burning up, unable to get where she was going, or do what she wanted to do. She meant to reach Cairo even if she had to walk.

'These things usually blow themselves out within twenty-four hours,' he told her. 'We'll be OK.'

'I hope so,' she said. 'We wouldn't get any refunds. This is one of those things in the Act-of-God clause, isn't it?'

He sat up. 'Of course they'd refund us. They'd have to.'

'I bet they wouldn't. It isn't their fault there's a sandstorm.'

'Well, it isn't mine, either.'

'Tough,' she said.

He got on the phone about it and tried to force a response out of the travel company. No one would give him a straight answer because so far nothing had gone wrong; but they seemed to be saying that if things did go wrong, then it wouldn't be up to them to indemnify anybody. In a case of delay the agency might – as a gesture of goodwill – be able to offer a day in a different country, but not an extra day in Egypt once the plane got there. He hung up.

'Told you,' she said.

'I guess they could send us to the Riviera. That might be nice.'

'It's freezing there. This is the coldest January they've had in Europe since 1948 or something like that.'

He put his arm around her and said he didn't care where he was, as long as he was with her.

She smiled back, feeling mean, unable to join him except by pretence. She knew already that she could never stay faithful to him. She'd been faithful to her first and second husbands, both when they were alive and after they'd died. But she could tell this was going to be different.

She honestly didn't love him, that was the trouble. And all at once she couldn't believe that she'd said yes, that she had the ring on her finger and was on her honeymoon. Why hadn't she just gone to bed with him and left it at that?

When they arrived, the air smelled hot and scorched, the sky was still laden with the aftermath of the storm: tiny particles that were invisible, but made it impossible to see clearly for very far. Lily didn't mind. She didn't mind anything, now that they were there.

Their hotel windows looked out on to two nineteenth-century villas set among palm trees. She was practically delirious with excitement. She didn't want to stay indoors and rest, or eat, or make love. She wanted to be outside, seeing everything.

He wasn't quite so enraptured. He hadn't realized it was going to be difficult to get his favourite brand of sourmash. And he said he thought the people were dark and dumpy.

'They're wonderful-looking,' she told him. 'Especially their faces. You aren't seeing them right. Why don't you like it here?'

'It doesn't seem all that romantic to me.'

'Wait till we get to the pyramids. We haven't even started.'

'I keep thinking what Ollie and Phil said about the flies. Sandflies everywhere.'

'But that's later in the year, not now.'

'And how sick they were with that gut-rot they picked up.'

'You won't pick up anything if you dress right. That's what my book says: wear a heavy sweater.'

'Not in the sun.'

'All the time. Dress like the locals, and you'll be all right.'

They went through the markets, where he was disappointed once more, because they couldn't find any sheets that were a hundred per cent cotton. The only ones on sale were cotton mixed with polyester; the rest had been exported.

But he liked the fact that she had calmed down. She held his hand now as they walked, where back home she had always seemed to be slipping her hand out of his. She smiled at him, saying, 'I love it here.' He said, 'And I love you.'

They began the tours. Straight away they were put into the middle of the place where all the pictures came from: the sphinx, the pyramids, the vast space full of chairs for the *son-et-lumière* show. She was trembling with eagerness. She almost seemed to be a little crazed. He whispered, 'Are you OK?' and she nodded vigorously, while motioning him with her hand to be quiet.

Their guide was a thin, grey-haired Austrian woman who had a thick accent. The other members of the troop were all American. Lily could see, as the guide took them from one spot to the next, how most of the little parties of tourists had been grouped according to nationality, so that the guides wouldn't have to repeat the same information in different languages; she wondered why their guide, Lisabette, had been chosen for an English-speaking group. Lisabette was definitely good at her job and made her subject sound interesting, but some of the others said afterwards that they were having trouble understanding her. Don said he'd heard her stating that one of the ancient characters on their list had had to 'accept the inedible'.

There were two old people in their group: Selma and Orville Potts. Selma had something to do with a cultural club back home. Orville was retired from the bank. They enjoyed everything and asked a lot of questions. They had also read a lot, unlike Don or the couple called Darrell – John and Patsy – who had a nine-year-old child in tow. The child's name was Cindy; she was orange-haired, freckled, and had white eyelashes and pale eyes. Despite the weak eyes, she was a determined starer. Selma had tried to make friends with the child, failed, and commented to the mother, Patsy, that, 'I reckon it's real nice for little Cindy to get let off school to go on vacation with you.' Patsy said, 'Oh, Cindy's between schools at the moment.' At the same time, John said, 'They've closed her school for a couple of weeks, to fix the pipes.'

'Well,' Selma said brightly, 'and are you having a good time?'

Cindy glared up at the old face peering down at her. Lily thought for a moment that the child was going to spit, but after a hesitation she muttered, 'Sure. It's OK.' Selma simpered. Cindy walked off, as if there were something a few feet away that she wanted to look at. Patsy and John seemed relieved.

Don and Lily moved ahead a few steps. They were followed by the other honeymoon couple, Ruth-Ann and Howie: she was tall, toothy and raucous; he was a tubby, high-voiced man. The idea of coming to Egypt had been his. Ruth-Ann didn't mind where she was, as long as they got away from the snow. She'd been thinking more of Hawaii, but this was fine. The only drawback was –

'No booze,' Howie complained.

'You're kidding,' Don said. 'You at some kind of Temperance hotel?'

'Oh, they've got a bar, but not like a real American bar. And no Jim Beam in the entire town, far as I can see.'

'You've got to bring it with you.'

'You're telling me,' Ruth-Ann said. 'We got so worried about rationing it for two whole weeks that we drank it all in the first three days. God, the hangovers we've had. It's like those stories about twenty people in a life-raft and only one canteen of water. What are you doing about it?'

'Well, we just got here,' Don said. 'I guess we'll measure it out in thimbles till the week is up, and then go on to wine. At least they still sell the stuff. I've heard they're thinking of making the whole country teetotal.'

Lily asked, 'Were you here for the sandstorm?'

'We sure were,' said Howie. 'We went to this hotel to meet a friend of Ruth-Ann's mother, and suddenly everything started to get dark, and then – wham! – they pulled all the shutters down, and we were stuck inside.'

'It can kill you,' Ruth-Ann said.

Lisabette was looking at her watch. It was almost time to start the tour again. Ruth-Ann said, 'Doesn't she look like something off of one of those tombs?'

Lily turned her head. Lisabette, small and emaciated, was adjusting the shoulderstrap of her bag. She still had her walking stick clenched to her, which made the operation more cumbersome. But when she finally straightened up, she put a hand to the piece of cloth wound around her head from the front to below the tight, grey bun at the back; she changed the stick over to her right side, then stood still. And it was true – she resembled some sort of ancient court official bearing a ceremonial staff.

'And what's the story with the kid?' Ruth-Ann murmured. 'Jesus, what an argument for birth-control.'

Howie sniggered. Lisabette raised her stick a few inches and looked up. Her nine listeners grouped around her again.

At the next break, most people took photographs. Lily hadn't thought about bringing a camera. She'd said she'd rather have a good postcard. But Don had brought along a small, cheap, foolproof camera. He told her, 'What I want are pictures of you.' He took two of her, then they changed places. She clicked the button twice, closed the slide over the lens and handed the camera back. She looked past him at one of the pyramids. 'The eternal triangles,' she said, and laughed.

'They aren't triangles. They've got five surfaces and the base is a squ—'

'For heaven's sake. I know that.' She turned away abruptly. She'd been careful for so long about not showing her true thoughts, that she was afraid to let out even a little irritation. When the outburst came, she might just start screaming, 'Oh Christ, you're so boring,' for half an hour. She was turning herself inside-out to entertain him and knocking herself out in bed to please him, just because she didn't love him enough.

And it wasn't his fault. He was a good, decent man; her mother was right. But it didn't make any difference. When she'd married before, both times, she'd been in love; she'd shared herself. Now she was only pretending. As a child, she'd loved playing make-believe. Now it wasn't for fun: now it was cheating.

She'd never be able to keep going. He'd be true to her – she was sure of him that way. And besides, he'd grown up in a family of ugly women who'd sat on him hard. The father had been the one with the looks, and had used them too, being unfaithful all over the place and finally leaving Don's mother. The mother and his two sisters looked like parodies of plain frontierswomen. They were also very concerned about all sorts of social, public and political issues that didn't interest Lily. They were the kind of women who would talk for hours about Vietnam at cocktail parties instead of getting married to somebody who'd die there. Don thought the way his sisters did, but he'd wanted to marry something different.

'What's wrong?' he said, hurrying up behind her.

'Nothing's wrong. I'm fine. She's going to start the spiel again, that's all.'

Lisabette raised her stick and brought it down on the ground. It made no noise, but the movement caught the attention of the rest of the group.

'You aren't mad at me, are you?' he said.

'Of course not.' She didn't take his arm or even look at him. She hated the way she was behaving.

'Egypt', Lisabette said, 'is a marriage between the Nile and the desert.' She began to talk about the importance of the periods of inundation and about the special regard paid to the androgynous deity of the Nile, Hapy. Lily's glance moved across the other tourists; it stopped at nine-year-old Cindy, whose fixed stare was boring into the back of Orville Potts; she suddenly felt a horror of the child. Something was wrong with Cindy. The parents obviously knew it, too. The mother was a nervous wreck. And the father – it was hard to tell: he wouldn't have had to live with the worry, the way the mother would. He'd only have to hear about it in the evenings and say, 'Yes, dear.'

Don reached out for Lily. She jumped as he touched her. He was trying to slide his hand up under her folded arms. She let him, since other people were there. If they'd been alone, she'd have pushed him away and walked off. She tried to concentrate on what Lisabette was telling them. Lisabette actually looked less like a living monument to ancient Egypt than like someone who'd once been alive and was now mummified; 'Hathor,' she said. 'The cow-goddess.'

Cindy grinned. Her eyes began to rove to other people. Lily moved her head and looked somewhere else.

On their way back to the bus, Howie said, 'You know what really turned me on to all this stuff? It was that big show from Tutankhamun's tomb.'

'Yes, I saw that, too,' Lily said.

Don pulled back on her hand. 'You did?' he asked. 'You never told me that.'

She shrugged. 'Me and about fifty million other people. Didn't you?'

'No, I missed it.'

'It was something,' Ruth-Ann told him. 'Talk about gorgeous – you can have all that Greek and Roman stuff.'

'Oh, I like that too,' Lily said. 'Only it never grabbed me the same way. It didn't have the philosophy.'

'The what?' Don asked.

'Haven't you been listening to what Lisabette's been saying?'

'Sure. All about the Nile god and the cow-goddess, and that kind of thing.'

'The first pyramids were built in steps, so the Pharaoh could go up there and into the sky and come back down again. After they died, they had their insides put into separate jars and they sailed across the sky in a boat. When they got to the other side, they went into the palace of death and answered all the questions about what kind of life they'd led. And if it was all right, then they started to sing chants to get back their stomach and brain and everything. The priest and the relatives of the dead person would help from back at the tomb. There were even little prayers for the heart, except that was the one thing they didn't take out. But I guess it had to be started up again. They called all the essential parts back into the body. And then the dead person would be whole in the other world.' She stopped, breathless.

'That isn't philosophy,' Don said.

'Hit him with your handbag,' Ruth-Ann told her.

'I'll hit him with the guidebook.'

'It still wouldn't make all that rigmarole philosophy.'

'Well, religion. I like the way they thought about people and animals and kings, and all the natural elements: all in one big lump.'

'They didn't think much of women, though,' Ruth-Ann said. 'You see these big statues of men, and way down near their feet is a tiny little figure of the wife – that's how unimportant they were.'

'No, it's just the opposite. The wife shouldn't be there at all. If you see one of those statues, it's really just supposed to represent the man, but he's specially asked to have his wife mentioned – for luck, or for sentiment. It's like nowadays, if a painter did a portrait of a businessman and the man insisted on taking a pose where he was holding a photograph of his wife. See? It's a gesture of affection. Nothing to do with despising anybody. They told us that in the museum lectures I went to.'

'There,' Howie said. 'They weren't so bad, after all.' He patted Ruth-Ann's behind lightly. She shooed him away. 'My wife's got this thing about victimized females.'

'My wife. He keeps saying it like that. I feel like I've lost my name all of a sudden.'

'I like the sound of it,' Howie said. 'I like trying it out. It's like driving around in a new car.'

Ruth-Ann climbed into the bus. 'Howie and his cars,' she said. Don followed. As Lisabette gave the driver the sign to start, he said to Lily, 'You should be hiring yourself out to one of these tourist outfits. I didn't realize you knew so much about the place.'

'I just went to all those lectures and I remember what they told us. You know how it is when you really like something.'

'Sure,' he said. 'I know how it is.' He put his arm around her again and she relaxed. She'd forgotten her irritation. She was glad to be with him and to have him holding her close to him.

That night she had a dream. It began like the dreams she'd had before leaving on the trip: she was standing under the blue sky, with the sun pouring down, and she was looking at the hiero-glyphics on the wall. But this time as she scanned the carvings, they began to form a story. The picture-writings seemed to be changing shape, running into each other and reforming. And after that, they became images that moved across the wall. It was like watching a film. In the picture-story she saw her first husband. He was standing on the bank of the river. Two servants were wrapping him in a length of white cloth that left him naked from the waist up. The material had been wound up into a long skirt. Then they continued. He raised his arms a little, while the men circled him with the bolt of material; they wrapped him to the midpoint of his chest, made him fold his arms, and proceeded to wind the cloth so that the arms were taped down.

She started to feel anxious. The place she was watching from began to draw nearer to the riverbank but she was still too far away to reach him. The long, white banner went around his neck. She could see they were going to bandage his face, too. She tried to call out, to move forward, to do anything to stop the men; but nothing worked. They wrapped her husband up completely, as if he'd been inside a cocoon. Only his legs, under the skirt, were free to walk. She looked on miserably until the work was finished.

The two men turned her husband around and walked him forward – one on each side – to the river, where a boat was waiting for them. As she saw him going away from her like that – entirely enclosed in white, and because of that seeming to be blind all over – she grew frantic. She screamed, but no one paid any attention to her. Her husband stepped forward into the boat. The servants guided him to the central part of the vessel, where a curtain hung. He went behind the curtain and she couldn't see him any more.

She wanted to go with him. She tried to run forward. The boat floated off, carrying him away. She tried to call out again, and again no one took any notice. She woke up. Don was kissing her in the dark. They began to make love before she realized that they were in their hotel room and that it was in Egypt.

The tour took them to the Valley of the Kings and the Valley of the Queens, the Tombs of the Nobles. Lily held their guidebook in one hand and talked as fast as a racetrack reporter about deities, animals, heavenly bodies, cults. Strange-sounding names flowed easily from her. Sometimes it seemed that in her zeal she was getting everything mixed up – that she was repeating a lot of misinformation, jumbling thoughts, condensing centuries, forgetting who the real people were and who were the gods.

Ruth-Ann said that if she tried for ten years, she was never going to be able to pronounce the name Hatshepsut. 'It's quite simple,' Lisabette told her. 'Hat-shep-sut. Repeat that.' Howie went off into a fit of giggles. Don said in a low voice that he found all of those names a little weird and couldn't remember any of them.

'That's because you didn't study them beforehand,' Lily said. 'If you don't know the names, how can you tell one god from another?'

'I can tell which one is supposed to be some animal. The cow-goddess and the jackal-god and the alligator-god.' He laughed. 'There's even a hippo-god, isn't there?'

'She's a goddess. She's a goddess of childbirth.'

'That figures. I guess they thought she had to be pregnant if she was so fat.'

'They didn't look at it that way.' She was beginning to get annoyed with him again. 'They thought that fat was a sign of abundance and good health.'

'And a high social standing,' Howie said. 'You can't stay overweight unless you keep up the food supply.'

'That's why the Nile was so important to them. They wouldn't have had any food without it.' The wind blew Lily's hair back, the sun was hot on her face. You could feel it was a genuine desert air. And now that all the dust had settled from the storm, the clarity – the light, was like nothing she'd ever imagined.

Ruth-Ann rejoined them. She said to Howie, 'Where's your sweater?'

'It's too hot.'

'You know what Lisabette told us: you'll pick up one of those bugs if you don't keep it on.'

'How could that help?'

'Well, she lives here. She ought to know.'

Lily teamed up with the Pottses, while Don got into a discussion with John Darrell. Orville and Selma – Selma especially – shared Lily's interest in Egyptian art and mythology. Ruth-Ann and Howie kept to themselves for a while, occasionally bursting into laughter. Once Lily heard Ruth-Ann pronounce 'Hatshepsut' again in a loud voice.

Lisabette concentrated on her three best students. Behind her shoulder, off in the distance, Patsy Darrell talked earnestly to her daughter; she'd come all the way around the world to do something she could have done at home – unless, possibly, the child was demanding the discussion in order to make sure that her mother didn't have the time to enjoy herself.

'I wish we were going to Saqqarah too,' Selma said, 'but we just don't have the time.'

'Never mind,' Lisabette told her. 'You will be fully satisfied by Karnak, I can assure you.'

'And Abu Simbel,' Orville said. 'I'm very interested in how they moved it. That must have been a magnificent feat of engineering.'

'And of international cooperation. It shows what can be accomplished when people work together in a spirit of peace.'

'And honesty,' Orville added. 'They tried to save Venice too. Pouring all that money into rescue funds – so now they've made about three people there into millionaires and the place is still sinking.'

'It's such a shame to have just one week,' Selma said. 'Well, a couple of days over a week.'

Lily agreed. She thought that she'd much rather go to Saqqarah than to Abu Simbel.

'It isn't on our tour,' Don told her. 'It's back where we came from.'

'We could change. Just go by ourselves one day.'

'If we took a whole day out, we might as well go to Alexandria.'

'But there isn't anything there.'

'There's a whole town.'

'There isn't anything old.'

'Lily, Abu Simbel's on the tour. You know it's going to be great. Haven't you seen the pictures?'

'Maybe we could stay on a little afterwards.'

'Our plane tickets—'

'Just a few days.'

'Maybe,' he said. 'We'll see.' He wouldn't say no outright. He didn't want to start an argument with her. She could see he was hoping that by the end of the week she'd have forgotten.

She walked back to the bus with Ruth-Ann, who told her, 'I was talking with Patsy back there. That's a real sick kid she's got. Jesus. She sets fire to things – I mean, like, houses. She isn't in school because – if you can believe it – she just burned it down. Honest to God. They keep moving all around. He's always got to find a new job, or get transferred.'

'Isn't there anything – doctors? Psychiatrists?'

'They're spending everything they've got on the doctors already. Her parents gave them the trip.'

Lily looked again at the Darrells, who were now standing near Lisabette. She wondered whether anything could help a child like Cindy. 'And they don't have any other children?' she said.

'I guess one was enough. A brat like that – I'm telling you: I'd sell her to the Arabs.'

'I don't know that the Arabs would like her any better than we do. I wonder if she was just born that way, or what?'

'You know what they say – some are born crazy, some become crazy and some have craziness thrust upon them. It all comes to the same thing in the long run.'

'Yes.'

'That's a real cute husband you've got there.'

Lily smiled. 'Want to trade?' she suggested.

Ruth-Ann shrieked with laughter. Howie came striding up to them, saying, 'What's she done – forgotten that name again?'

That night Lily had the dream again. She stood in front of the wall, stared at the writing, and it started to turn into pictures that told her a story. It was the same story, but this time the man being prepared for the ride in the boat was her second husband. She watched, as before: at the beginning surprised and touched to see him, and wanting to walk up and talk to him; then, when it was too late, desperate to be heard – trying to stop the others from taking him away. And she woke up again.

'What's wrong?' Don whispered.

'Dream,' she said.

'I thought you were in pain. You were making noises.'

'No, it's all right.'

'Maybe I'd better check everything, just to make sure. Does this feel all right?'

She put her arms around him and said that felt fine; and there, and that, too.

They went to Karnak. As Lily stepped into the ferry, she remembered her dream; but this was a modern craft, whereas the one in her dream had been like the ones on the frescoes, ancient.

They both loved Karnak. Don took a lot of photographs and Lily changed her mind about the camera. She became interested in trying to get pictures of the undersides of the overhead stone beams. The intensity of light around them was so great that it was thrown up, illuminating the colours on the surfaces high over their heads.

'This place is gigantic,' Don said. 'I've never seen anything like it.' He and Howie and Orville moved off together, leaving Ruth-Ann with Lily. Selma wanted Lisabette to look at something in her guidebook. Patsy, as usual, stayed at a distance from the rest of them, keeping watch over Cindy. John started to walk towards the group of men.

'Those two,' Ruth-Ann said.

'Patsy and John?'

'Patsy and her child-arsonist.'

'Poor woman. What can she do? All of a sudden when they're five, you find out you've got a bum one – you can't take it back to the store. She's stuck with that, I guess.'

'And so's he.'

Lily looked at the men. She noticed that Howie was in his shirtsleeves. All the others had on sweaters or jackets. John was gesturing up at the columns. 'I don't know,' she said. 'He might walk out any time now. What do you think?'

'Oh? I guess it's possible. She can't have much time for him if she's got her hands full like that. Did you hear what happened when we were getting into the boat? Cindy said something to Selma.'

'What?'

'I didn't hear. But I've never seen such a reaction. Selma and Orville, too. Then the two of them started to say something to Patsy and she blew up. John tried to calm them all down. And that horrible, rat-faced kid just looked smug.'

'I wonder what it was.'

'Something mean, I bet.'

Later in the day, Selma came and sat next to Lily. They talked about the ruins. Lily admired the other guidebook, which was larger than her own, and full of coloured pictures. 'I'll give it to you when we leave,' Selma said. 'I bought two, because I knew the one I'd be carrying around was bound to get all tattered. Just tell me the name of your hotel in Cairo and I'll drop it off there. If you don't mind it in this condition.'

'I'd love it,' Lily told her.

'I'll tell you something, though: a lot of the information in it is different than we're being told. Sometimes the change is just very slight, and sometimes it really contradicts what the book says. Makes you wonder.'

'How?'

'Well, you know those two statues of the king on his throne? Here's the picture.'

'The husband and wife in their chairs. Sure. The ones that had the singing heads till the nineteenth-century restorers filled them up.'

'That's just it. That's so far from what the guidebook says that you could suspect she just made it up. First of all, both of those figures are the king: Amenhotep III. Then, it says here that one of them, the north one, was so badly damaged in the earthquake of 27BC that part of it cracked and fell. And that was the one that became famous for singing – because the sun used to heat up the cracks, or the wind got into it or something. But all that was way, way back. It was written about by the Romans. And the Romans restored the statue two hundred years or so after it was broken. So, Lisabette's story about how they were built that way in the first place – it just doesn't make sense. That's what she said, wasn't it – that they were part of the sun-worship?'

They were, Lisabette had told them, embodiments of conjugal love; although the seated figures represented a great king and queen, who were the guardians of their people, they were also just like anyone else: a husband and wife. They too obeyed natural laws and worshipped the gods. When the sun-god reached the horizon in his boat and prepared to sail across the sky, they would welcome him, praising him with their voices.

'They sang,' Lisabette had said. 'They were constructed as musical instruments. A work of genius.' Their heads were hollow, carved inside with a system of intricately fluted trails and passageways. When the morning sun struck their foreheads, its heat activated the air within and made the stone sing – not singing according to a melody, but long, sustained notes that changed tone as the light grew stronger. In the last century, in order to preserve them, the statues were repaired, the heads filled with cement. And now they no longer made a sound. The two giant figures stared straight ahead, waiting for the sun, silent.

'Did you ask her about it?' Lily said.

'I told her my guidebook talked about reconstruction by Septimus Severus, and all that.'

'And?'

'And she said that a lot of these books used different sources.'

'That's probably true, isn't it?'

'But not that true. Not so you'd make a mistake like that. And anyway, you can certainly see they're both men – not a married couple.'

'I think I like her version better.'

'No, dear. Not if it's fictitious. The truth is always better.'

'If you can tell what it is.'

Selma sighed and said how strange it was to be in a modern country whose whole appearance was still dominated by the culture of its past. Cairo was a modern city, to be sure, but so much of Egypt seemed the same as in ancient days. Yet it wasn't the same, naturally. The only country left where you could say the past and present were still the same was India: she'd always wanted to go there, but Orville had this ridiculous feeling against it. He wouldn't go. 'All the methods of making things, the craftsmanship, is still the same there,' she said. 'They still wear the same clothes. But above all, what makes the real difference is that they still believe in and practise the same religions. And that's all gone here.'

Lily said yes, and thought again about the two statues. She looked up into the huge gatework of sunlit, painted stone, down at the canyoned pathways in shadow. 'You can still feel it, though,' she said. 'Especially in a place like this.'

'Yes indeed. It's like the travel people said: you can almost imagine the gods walking here.'

Lily remembered the Englishwoman who lived in the house that was supposed to be dedicated to Isis. 'There's something I've got to ask Lisabette before I forget,' she said.

'Make sure you check it in a book afterwards. Unless it's something about herself. Now that's a tragic story. She told me her father was killed in the First World War, her first husband and her brother died in the Second World War and her son was killed in the June War.'

'I guess that's one of the things that lasts longer than religions,' Lily said. 'People killing each other.'

'I've never heard of one person having so much bad luck. Orville said how did I know she hadn't just concocted the story about her sad personal history – that's what he said: concocted. But I can't believe it. No. You can see she's had sorrows in her life. Maybe they've driven her to – you know, sort of invent things. Well, not really. They wouldn't hire somebody who did that. I expect she exaggerates a little, that's all.'

Lily got to her feet. She said the thing about bad luck was that no matter what kind it was, a little went a long way.

She found Lisabette standing in the shade, not far from Orville and Ruth-Ann. 'I wonder if you can help me,' she began.

Lisabette moved her head stiffly. 'Yes?'

'I've heard about an Englishwoman who lives in Egypt – I think maybe in Cairo – in a house she thinks used to belong to a priestess of Isis. I wondered if you'd know anything about her. Or even about the house.'

'No, I've never heard of this.'

'It was on the radio. She did excavation work on the house and found the garden, and that kind of thing.'

'I don't know of such a person.'

'Could you tell me where I could go to find out?'

'Possibly the embassy?'

Of course, Lily thought. She should have figured that out herself. The woman had been working with the British archaeological teams; the embassy would know how to get in touch with them.

'Isis?' Ruth-Ann said behind her shoulder. 'She's the one that cut off her husband's prick and grew him again from it. That's some trick, huh?'

'It's one of the great pagan myths,' Lisabette said curtly.

'And how.'

'Containing profound observations on the nature of death, sacrifice and regeneration, life after death, and the power of love.'

'And bereavement,' Lily said. Lisabette's eyes met hers. The old woman's face lost its lecture-look; it lapsed into a softer expression that made her appear even older and more exhausted. It reminded Lily of the way Don's small, ugly, buck-toothed mother had looked when she'd wished them both a happy marriage and added that her own wedding day had been the happiest day of her life.

'Just so,' Lisabette said.

On the way back from Karnak there was a quarrel among the other passengers, or perhaps a continuation of whatever had already started between the Darrells and the Pottses. In the stark, offended silence that followed, Howie's voice could be heard announcing that he didn't feel well; he was sure it was the restaurant they'd been to the night before: the lousy, contaminated food they served you in this country. Lisabette threw a lizardlike look over the back of her seat and told him without sympathy that he shouldn't have taken off his pullover while the wind was still blowing so strongly – it was no wonder he'd caught something.

'I really do feel pretty bad,' he said a few more times. By the end of the ride he looked almost green in the face. As they left the ferry, Ruth-Ann told Lily and Don that if Howie had to change their travel arrangements, this would be goodbye, but she wanted to say it had been nice to meet them. Everyone offered to help. Ruth-Ann shook her head. She'd ask the hotel, she said; they'd find her a doctor if Howie needed one.

Late that evening Lily said that she wanted to go to Abydos and Saqqarah. And they should be staying on the other bank anyway, in Luxor.

'I guess we'll have to leave them for another trip,' Don told her.

'When do you think we'd ever get back? It's such a long way from home. Doesn't it make more sense to go now, when we're here?'

'We just don't have the time, honey.'

'And at Luxor: the temple. We're right here on the spot.'

'We can't. We—'

She stood up and delivered a tirade about the importance of beauty to the development of a culture. He didn't know what she was talking about, and he didn't think she understood half of what she was saying, but in the end he agreed to change all their plans, so that they'd be able to get back to Luxor. Abydos was out, he declared. If she got Luxor, he'd be allowed Abu Simbel.

She then wanted to start telephoning the British embassy to

find out where to get hold of the priestess of Isis. 'Later,' he told her: after they got back from the next day's sightseeing.

On their way out in the morning, the man at the desk handed Lily a package – a book wrapped in a piece of hotel writing paper that was held tight by a rubber band. On the paper was a short note from Selma, saying that they too had changed plans and were going to visit a shrine somewhere out in the desert. The book was the guidebook she'd promised to let Lily keep.

Lily's pleasure in the book was the only sign that she still considered the world worth noticing. She read while standing, sitting or walking. She read the book all through the journey to Abu Simbel and parts of the actual tour. She was in such a bad mood that Don was almost frightened for her.

They had said goodbye to Lisabette and the Darrells. Now they were with a larger group, of sixteen people: Americans, Australians, Britons and South Africans. Their guide was a young man named Franz, who came from a part of Switzerland that was mainly German-speaking. His accent was a good deal better than Lisabette's, but he had a rapid-fire delivery that left many of his hearers mystified, especially when he reeled off lists of ancient deities or rulers.

During one of the breaks when they were supposed to wander around by themselves or take their photographs, Don sat down next to Lily. He tried to coax the guidebook from her. She dodged away. He dropped something into her lap. 'What's that?' she asked.

'A lucky stone. It's got a ring around it.'

'Stones don't last long in the desert,' she said. 'They all turn to sand.' She picked the stone out of her lap and threw it away. It bounced off the side of a larger stone and fell into a heap of pebbles. The bright light made it indistinguishable from the other shapes around the place where it had landed.

'I ought to hit you,' he said.

'Go ahead. Go right ahead.'

'You won't take anything from me, will you?'

It was true. She wanted to scream with rage, or get up and start running, or hit him first. She'd never treated anyone so badly. She was ashamed of herself, but she couldn't quit. She even wondered if she'd married him because – believing that there was a curse on her – she'd been willing to let him die. She also realized that although she couldn't accept his love, she wanted him to keep on caring. Her resistance to him was like a lack of faith, an atheistic impulse; if there were suddenly nothing against which to fight, she might be completely lost.

'Christ, what I'd like to do to you,' he said.

She thought he really was going to hit her, but he turned and stormed off in the direction of the river. He stood looking out at the water, with his back to her.

She felt tears of stubbornness and remorse rising in her eyes. Her throat ached. But she was also proud at the way he was standing up to her. If he could hold out like that, he might win her over and exorcize the curse. Or maybe it had nothing to do with him; it might be more important that she should talk with the priestess of Isis.

That night, as they were getting ready to go to bed, Lily said, 'I wonder where the others are now – if Howie's all right.'

'He'll be fine. People don't die of a stomach ache.'

'I wonder what the quarrel was about. The one between Selma and that horrible little girl.'

'What are any quarrels about?'

'Well, I guess each one's different.'

'Your mother warned me about you, you know.'

'Great,' she said. 'That's the kind of mother to have. OK, what did she say?'

'Oh, never mind.'

'You can't leave it there. If you don't tell me, I'll call her up long distance, right this minute.' Her mother; suddenly it was like having another person along on the honeymoon. Her mother envied her the two widowings. They were even more romantic and dramatic than Ida's divorce.

'She said you thought there was a curse on you.'

'Oh?'

'Well?'

'Well, I sometimes feel like that, yes.'

She got into the bed, taking the guidebook with her, but when he reached towards the lamp, she put the book on the night-table. He turned out the light. She waited in the darkness for him to go on with the conversation.

At last he said, 'You never talk about the others.'

'What others?' she whispered.

'The other two.'

She didn't answer.

'Your husbands,' he said.

There was a silence again, longer than the first one.

'What for?' she asked.

'It's something important in your life.'

She rolled to the side, to get near the edge of the bed. He put out his arm and pulled her back.

'It was a long time ago,' she said. 'They both were. I don't remember. And I don't want to. When people die, you get over it by moving forward.'

'And I guess some people never get over it.'

'I don't know.'

I don't know what other people remember, she thought, *but I remember everything – every room we were in, every place. Love does that; everything new, fun, easy to remember. It was the only time I felt I was living. I just can't talk about it, that's all.*

'If I died, you'd move forward?' he asked.

'That's a dumb thing to say. Besides, you had girlfriends before you met me.'

'I was never married.'

'It amounts to the same.'

'No, it doesn't. It's completely different.'

'I don't think so.'

He said, 'I used to have this idea that you were like one of those maidens in the fairytales, who had to have the spell broken.'

'And what do you think now?'

'I think maybe you don't love me very much.'

Here it comes, she thought. But no, he wouldn't really believe that. He'd just want her to say: *Of course I do.*

She said, 'You don't have any reason to think that. It's because I get into bad moods, isn't it?'

He stretched and shifted his weight, moving his arm an inch higher under her back. He said, 'Well, not exactly.'

His voice sounded faint and sad. Suddenly she was weeping uncontrollably. 'Of course I love you,' she sobbed. 'Of course I do.'

Their time was running out. They could go back to Cairo and enjoy the town for a day, or they could see one other site and hurry back. Lily held the guidebook tightly and said that she absolutely needed to see Abydos and Edfu and Bubastis and

Saqqarah: and after that, they had to have a few days extra in Cairo so that she could find the priestess of Isis.

'Say all that again,' he told her.

'The sanctuary of Abydos and the sacred lake of—'

'No: the priestess part.'

She told him about the Englishwoman who lived in Cairo and believed herself to be the incarnation of an ancient priestess of Isis.

He said, 'Listen, you really want to see some old crone suffering from delusions? Didn't you notice, we've got plenty of those at home?'

'We don't have the temple of Isis or the house of the priestess.'

'Well, we can ask somebody, I guess.'

'I asked Lisabette. She hadn't heard of her.'

'That settles it.'

'She said I should try the embassy.'

'Oh?'

'I did. When you went to see about the tickets. But I don't think I got hold of the right people. Nobody knew. They gave me a lot of names of different people and they turned out to be away on trips. But all I need to do is wait. Lots of people must have heard of her if she was on the radio.'

'I'm not going to spend all the time we've got left, trying to track down some old woman. She's probably died by now, anyway. Why do you want to see her?'

Lily didn't know. There wasn't any reason, just the desire. She tried to think of something to tell him.

'I want to see her because she, um, lives in that place.'

'Where?'

'Well, it's an ancient Egyptian house, with a garden in it. And anyhow, she's the priestess of Isis. That's why I want to see her.'

'We just don't have the time.'

'I want to stay,' she said. 'To stay here longer.'

'Of course you can't stay. I've got to get back to the office.'

Now he'd be saying to himself: who's footing the bill for all this? *Well*, she thought, *he offered*. She took a firm grip on the guidebook and looked up into his eyes. 'You can get back to the office,' she suggested. 'And I could stay on here for a while.'

'No.' He said it so loudly that a cluster of other guests in the hotel lobby turned around to look.

'Just a few—'

'Don't push your luck, Lil,' he said. He stared at her so fiercely that he looked almost frightening, but also exciting. She leaned forward and put her hands on his arms, turned her face upward.

He grabbed hold of both her hands and began to pull her across the floor to the elevator. A group of people were standing in front of the doors. He started to drag her around the corner and up the stairs. 'What's wrong?' she said. 'Where are we going?'

'Upstairs,' he answered.

'What for?'

'It's the only place I can get any sense out of you.'

She tried to kiss him on the neck and sat down in the middle of the staircase. He piled on top of her, laughing. A woman's voice from below them called, 'Hello, hello, you two. Did you drop this?'

They turned their heads. Down at the bottom of the staircase stood a woman who was smiling broadly. She was holding the guidebook in her right hand and waving it back and forth.

By mid-morning they were on their way to the ruins. Don seemed to be dozing behind his sunglasses. Lily sat quietly, the book held primly in her lap as if it might have been a prayer-book. Their new touring companions included two burly, grey-haired men – one Dutch and the other Irish – who were travelling together; an old Canadian woman on her own; and an American family of five: father, mother, two well-developed teenaged daughters and a son of about twelve. The son was interested in the height, width, and exact measurements of all the parts of every building they saw. He told Franz, the group in general and then Don in particular, that he'd worked out a theory about pyramidology that explained just everything you'd ever want to know. His two sisters had their eyes on Franz; the younger one, called Tina, was dressed – foolishly, so her mother told her – in a white T-shirt and red shorts. 'They aren't shorts,' the girl objected. 'They're hot pants.' The older sister, Lucille, was more conservative; she had on a pair of long trousers and a matching jacket.

Lily moved away from Don early in the tour. She told him that she wanted to read up on a few things. She sat down and looked out into the distance. Behind her people were taking photographs. The older American girl came up to where Lily was sitting; her face still covered by the camera, she said, 'This is just great. Isn't it great?'

'Mm.'

'The lure of the ancient world – I was always nuts about that kind of thing.' She said that what had really convinced her parents had been her brother's insistence on his theory; he was going to make it his school topic for the coming term. She too had been thinking about Egypt for years, having been extremely impressed by an opera she'd once been taken to: Egyptian dress and scenery had figured prominently among the memorable aspects of the production. The name of the composer escaped her at the moment, though she hummed a little of her favourite tune from it, which she said was called 'The Nuns' Chorus From Aida'.

Lily said that was nice; her own introduction had been through the museums.

Yes, the girl told her, they were OK, but you had to get outdoors to see what was left of the buildings: she liked the temples and things best. She liked, she said, as she moved away with the camera, the way they'd built everything on such a big scale.

Lily closed the guidebook. She felt that she wanted to stay where she was for a long time, just sitting and doing nothing. She remembered a day at home, a few years back, when she'd gone for a walk in the park. It had been an afternoon in the fall – the distances full of hazy sunshine, the leaves gold, brown, coppery. Two young mothers had been sitting on a bench in front of hers. Each of them had a baby carriage nearby. Sometimes nurses and babysitters came to the park but these girls, she'd felt sure, were the real mothers. And something about the scene, or the season, or maybe just the weather, had made her think what a waste it was that people had only one life, that the choices were always so few, that you couldn't lead several lives all at once or one after the other.

But now it seemed to her that what remained of the past was just as much where she belonged as was the present. In fact, you couldn't help living more lives than one. Thought took you into other times. And there was always going to be so much to see and learn: you could never reach the end of it.

Don came and sat down beside her. 'That kid's obsessed,' he said. 'Another one.'

'Numerology?'

'Everything except spacemen. He thinks they had astronomical observatories and balloon flight and just about everything.'

'I think the real facts are more interesting.'

'The reincarnation of priestesses – that kind of thing?'

'Like the fact that all the lower-class people had broken teeth from eating stone-ground bread. Everyone I've ever met who's had a thing about health-food bread has chipped a tooth at least once.'

'Is that in the guidebook?'

'That was in the lectures. They also told us: the men who worked in the mummifying business were divided into different classes, too. And the ones that handled all the poor people's trade considered it a privilege of the profession that they should be allowed to have sexual intercourse with the corpses.'

'You're kidding.'

'Apparently it's a well-known thing.'

'Of course they were completely dominated by the idea of death.'

'Most cultures are. Don't you like all this?'

'Sure. It's terrific. But I'm going to be glad to get back.'

'Snow and ice?'

'This is fine for a time. But you know what it is.'

'It's history.'

'It's a graveyard.'

'So's most of history. They lived a long time ago. And all that's left is what survived. This is here because it's stone. The houses where they lived were made out of wood and mud and plastery stuff. So, they're all gone. The tombs and temples – the religious side of life – they were built to last. It's not so different nowadays; most old churches are made out of stone.'

'Uh-huh.' He took the guidebook out of her lap and flipped through the pages. 'Franz says he's going on to Abydos with the group.'

'Good. That's one of the most sacred places.'

'It's too far away. It's got to be someplace nearer. We'd just have time to make Saqqarah, if you wanted to. I'd rather go straight back to Cairo and not have to rush so much.'

'OK,' she said. 'Saqqarah.' She breathed in and stood up, saying, 'It's so clean here. The light's so wonderful. And the air – you can understand why some people decide they want to go off into the desert and never come back.'

'Would you ever do that?'

'Not without a guidebook,' she said, taking it back from him.

They strolled towards the others. Don said, 'This is another funny bunch, though. We seem to end up with the oddballs.'

'The family's nice.'

'But a little weird.'

'I don't think so.'

'That boy?'

'That's just getting carried away by his ideas. And I liked the older girl. She loves everything about the place.'

'I think maybe her sister's the one that's going to get Franz.'

'Oh, no. If anybody's going to get Franz, I'd put my money on the mother.'

He laughed and took her free hand. They were in tune for the rest of the day: all during the trip back to their hotel, through the evening and night, for the next leg of their journey and on their arrival at the new hotel.

In the morning they started to quarrel. It happened so fast that before either one of them knew what had led to it, he was hissing at her, 'The minute you get out of bed, it's all gone. All I get is that silence. It's like you can't stand to be near me. You don't even look at me. You'd be that way in bed with anybody, wouldn't you?'

She wouldn't answer back. She just continued to put her clothes on, trying to keep out of his way in the small room.

He came up to her and turned her around. 'Tell me about them,' he said. 'Tell me about the other two.'

She plunged away, furious, and said, 'No.' If it was going to turn into a real fight, she was all set to pick up an ashtray or a lamp and throw it at him. She went on getting dressed.

They didn't speak to each other on the way to the site, or when they got there. They sat or stood side by side, enraged and indignant. No one noticed anything wrong because, for the first time, they were in a large group of tourists – nearly twenty people – who didn't seem to have been brought together before. There was no chatting among the crowd. The guide was an Egyptian woman of studious appearance, who might have been a teacher or lecturer on the off-season. Her voice was rather soft, which meant that her audience had to crowd up close, to be sure not to miss anything.

They saw the frescoes, heard about the cult of the bull, passed by one of the most famous pyramids. The ancient Egyptians, they were reminded, called every pyramid 'the house of eternity'; the king's statue would be seated inside, looking out on to the world through peepholes. If the statue was there, the king was there. The work of art had a purpose beyond mere decoration: it was a stand-in.

They walked in the direction of a huge mound of building rubble that looked like another, unfinished, pyramid. Lily had forgotten which places were ancient and which had been left by the excavators. Her strength began to recede as they neared the base of the structure. She thought how pointless her whole life had turned out to be. It was no use trying to fight bad luck; some people just had that deal from the deck. To consider marriage for a third time had been foolish beyond comprehending. She didn't feel that she could ever possibly get to know him, or that she'd want to; and she was suddenly so tired that she was ready to lie down in the sand and stay there.

He grabbed her hand. She looked back over her shoulder for the others; they'd gone somewhere else with the guide.

He started to tug her along the ground, yanking her hard by the arm. And he began to yell abuse at her. He was dragging her towards the pyramid-like hill – she couldn't imagine why. He said that she could damn well pull herself together and take an interest in their future and be a little nice to him sometimes and show that she appreciated it when he gave in to her – because that was what he was always having to do, all the time, and never getting any thanks for it, either.

When they came to the beginnings of stonework, he started to climb up, hauling her along with him. She had to follow. If she tried to sit down, she'd be cut and bruised. She called out for him to wait, but he wouldn't. 'You're hurting my arm,' she said. He climbed higher, taking her with him, until she thought her arm was going to twist out of her shoulder. And all at once he stopped, sweating, and faced her. He let go of her hand.

'You know what else your mother said?' he told her. 'She said maybe it was a blessing in disguise that your first two husbands died so soon, before they found out what a spoiled bitch you really are.'

She stepped back. She felt the sun shining on the top of her head, but she was cold. It was like the time when she'd lost her lucky-piece: the same terror. A few voices from below came up to her.

'Oh Jesus, Lily,' he said. 'I'm sorry.'

She took another step back. She still wasn't able to answer, though her eyes hadn't moved from his face.

'Look out,' he said suddenly.

She turned, knew that she was slipping and saw her foot skidding over the edge. She started to fall. He grabbed her by her skirt and slid past her. They tumbled downward for several yards and stopped a few feet apart. More voices came up from below them, shouting loudly.

Lily picked herself up carefully. Her knees and shins were scraped, her left elbow and forearm were bleeding. Otherwise, she seemed to be all right. She crawled over to where Don had fallen. He was lying on his back, looking up at her. She sat down beside him.

He said, 'I didn't mean it.'

'It doesn't matter.'

'Are you all right?' he asked.

'I'm fine.'

He said, 'I can't move.'

She called down to the people standing below. She screamed for them to bring help. They said that they were coming; several of them started up the rock surface.

She touched his cheek with her fingers and took his hand in hers. He smiled a little. Soon after that, he died. She was still holding his hand, so she felt and saw the moment when it happened. She hadn't been able to be with her first two husbands when they'd died.

At the airport both mothers were waiting: hers and his. Her mother began to cry straight away, loudly announcing, 'Oh, poor Lily – I thought this time it had to be all right. But it wasn't meant to be.'

Lily gave her a brief hug, pushed her aside and walked on, to where Don's mother stood. Lily embraced her, finding it strange that the one who was the mother should be the small one. 'I was with him,' she said. 'He wasn't in pain at all.' Her mother-in-law nodded. Lily said, 'It was so quick. He asked me if I was all right. He was thinking of me, not of himself. And then he just went.' She started to cry. Her mother-in-law too, wept. And behind her, her mother sobbed noisily, still saying that she'd been so sure everything was going to work out this time; that she couldn't believe *it had happened again*.

The funeral was down in the country at his mother's place, where they'd had the wedding reception. As Lily walked out of the front door and over to the car, she remembered the other time: when she'd emerged with Don from the identical doorway, to get into the car that was to carry them to their future as husband and wife.

She asked her mother-in-law if she could stay with her for a while. The two of them took walks together in the snow. Lily began to see more of her sisters-in-law; it was a large family and a lot of them lived near enough to turn up for Sunday lunch.

She kept expecting to have the same dream about Don that she'd had about her other husbands: to see him being dressed in the winding-sheet and taken away in the boat. But she had stopped having dreams.

She was pregnant. She told her mother-in-law first. And she was thankful that her sister was planning to remarry near the end of September, so that her mother's attention would be deflected from her at the crucial time.

The child was born: a boy. She couldn't sleep. She couldn't concentrate on anything else. She forgot the pain and regret she had felt about not having been able to love her husband. The business of being a mother was harder than anyone had led her to believe. It was exhausting to the limit of her patience, and at times so far beyond that she didn't think she was going to get through it.

One day she looked at her son as he stood aside from a group of children he was playing with. He reminded her suddenly of a photograph she had that showed her grandfather at the same age; and also, she realised, of Don: the resemblance was so startling that it was almost like a reincarnation.

She confessed to her mother-in-law that she thought she hadn't loved Don enough – not as much as he'd deserved.

Her mother-in-law said, 'That's the way people always feel. But I know you loved him. Anyone can see what a good mother you are.'

She didn't think she was such a good mother. She thought she was slapdash and nervous, constantly fussing. The only thing she was sure of was that she loved her son. And she was delighted and extremely surprised that her father, who had always seemed hopeless as far as family matters were concerned, had fallen in love with the child: he'd turn up on the doorstep to take the boy for a ride, or to play outdoors somewhere, or to go on a trip to the zoo; they had private jokes together and stories that they told each other. She began to be fond of her father again, as she had been when she was young.

One day a reporter wanted to interview her. Her statements were to be included in a programme about war widows, which was going to be broadcast as a companion-piece to a documentary that dealt with veterans. The compilers planned to talk to children, too. They seemed irritated that Lily hadn't had any children by her first two husbands.

She told them that she was happy. It hadn't been easy, she said, and it had taken a long time, but she'd had a lot of help. She praised her mother-in-law.

Even if she'd been in the mood for it, she hardly had the time to dream. But she often remembered Egypt. One picture especially came back to her from the trip: of two immense statues made of stone – each out of a single piece – that were represented seated on chairs; the figures were sitting out in the middle of nowhere, side by side and both looking in the same direction: east, towards the sunrise. Sometimes she thought about them.